I0690183

LEATHERDADDY

First Edition

Published by The Nazca Plains Corporation
Las Vegas, Nevada
2009

ISBN: 978-1-935509-46-2

Published by

The Nazca Plains Corporation ®
4640 Paradise Rd, Suite 141
Las Vegas NV 89109-8000

PUBLISHER'S NOTE
Leatherdaddy is a work of fiction created wholly by *G.W. Leatherman Parks'* imagination. All characters are fictional and any resemblance to any persons living or deceased is purely by accident. No portion of this book reflects any real person or events.

Cover Photo
Fleshblack www.fleshblack.be

Art Director
Blake Stephens

DEDICATION

I have been a proud member of the Leather community for over thirty years. I wear my Leathers proudly on a daily basis. I have had the honor of meeting many amazing Leathermen who stand tall and proud in their Leathers including Michael Eisenblatter, my oldest and dearest Leatherfriend, Tom M. and Jim H., and Steve S., all of whom have supported me as members of our proud tribe. I am grateful to Jim Maciel, President and Founder of F.L.A.G. for giving me the opportunity of publishing my Leather stories in the organization's newsletter, FLAGSHIP. Many of the stories in this volume initially appeared in that newsletter. I am extremely grateful to two mentors, Alex Ironrod and Tim Brough, for their encouragement in seeking the publication of this anthology. Lastly, I am grateful to the boys carl, chris and most especially jim, who have willingly served as submissives, allowing me to build on my repertoire of S&M activity.

LEATHERDADDY

First Edition

Erotic Literature by the Black Leather Gloved Hands of

G.W. Leatherman Parks

CONTENTS

CONTENTS CONTINUED

THE UNIFORM'S CHRISTENING

The uniform conveniently arrived on a Friday.

As I opened the box, the smell of black Leather was overpowering and I couldn't help but bury my face in it, inhaling the strong, masculine smell that new Leather has. God, it was overpowering and the bulge in my pants was instant.

Black Leather shirt with white piping accenting the epaulets, the pockets and the sleeves. The pants had a corresponding stripe down the legs. The best part was the codpiece, with a white stripe down the center. It would encase my cock and balls and I knew it would be filled on more than one occasion with my excited manrod.

I couldn't get up the steps fast enough to strip off my business suit and the other trappings of the white collar shit world I inhabited by day. Leatherman by night.

As I pulled on the pants they caressed my legs as if a boy with a velvet tongue was licking them. That would happen soon enough.

The shirt was tight, the cuffs encircling my upper arms. I couldn't resist putting on nipple clamps which strained against the Leather fabric.

My Dehners slipped on over the tight Leather legs of the pants.

Final touches – tight Damascus gloves and my Muir cap.

Fuck, I was hot.

I had to strut my stuff.

With my mirrored sunglasses in place, I looked like the fucking hottest cop as I walked the few blocks to the Leather bar.

It was early, there were only a few guys milling around, but I was instantly the center of attention.

Most of the guys wore tee shirts and jeans, but I knew as the night advanced more Leathermen were due to arrive. I picked up my beer and retreated to the private section of the bar where the bartender and owner looked the other way as men lighted up their smokes. I settled into a corner of the bar, patiently waiting for an appropriate boy. I lighted a cigar.

As I puffed on my cigar, a handsome young Leatherman made his appearance. Sizing him up, I couldn't quite tell if he was a top or a bottom.

Actually, it didn't matter to me – there were quite a few 'tops' that I had conquered. I observed him through my mirrored glasses.

Nice-looking. Trim body.

Faded blue jeans. Tight chaps outlining his basket. As he turned, no hankies in the back pocket to suggest his orientation. No keys suspended from a D ring.

He wore a Muir cap, a Leather shirt and a motorcycle jacket. Wescos to the knee.

My cock was excited. He fit the profile of a Leatherman that interested me.

I continued to puff on the cigar and suck on my beer as he pulled out a large cigar.

I sauntered over and lighted his cigar for him.

"Thanks, Buddy."

"You're welcome... I'm G.W."

"I'm Mike."

We chatted for a few minutes and I knew that I wanted to take him back to my place. Work him over. But he made no motions of a similar nature.

More guys were filtering in but none had the same Leather persona that this guy had.

As we talked, I slowly massaged my cod. But he made no efforts to take over that duty.

He continued to make small talk, but I was losing interest. I wanted to get sucked and if he wasn't going to do it, someone else would have to. The uniformed Leatherman was horny.

Abruptly, he excused himself and headed to the entrance of the private section where a man in full Leather had just made his appearance. Mike knelt in front of him and nuzzled the newly-arrived man's crotch area.

"Ah," I thought to myself, "he is someone else's boy.... Shit!"

The newly-arrived guy was handsome with a heavy black beard and mustache. It complimented his full black Leather outfit.

I watched as the Master held the boy's face in place in his crotch. The boy's arms encircled the man's legs as he continued to massage the man's crotch with his face. I wanted it to be my crotch. I fondled my already-erect cock in its Leather pouch.

"Ah, shit..." I thought again.

After some time, the Leatherman pulled his boy's head away and gestured for the boy to rise. They began a heavy passionate kissing.

I finished my beer and as I walked past to order another one, the Leatherman interrupted his kissing, turned to me and whispered. "You're one damned hot fucker... hang around."

"I'll be back, just going to get a beer."

I was intrigued. Got my beer. Came back to the area – they were still engaged in fondling and kissing.

When the Leatherman saw me return, however, he once again interrupted his activity and followed me, pulling his boy with him.

After introducing myself, he introduced himself as Steve. We conversed. All the time Mike stood silently by.

Steve was handsome too. He packed his ass-tight Leathers well. Fuck, I thought, I wouldn't mind having my cock in his mouth.

"You ever play with a twosome?" Steve asked.

"On occasion."

"You got a playroom?"

"Yes, I only live a few blocks away..."

"What are you into?"

"Bondage, flogging..."

"Any playtime available tonight?"

"Sure, we can work your boy over..."

"Let's rock and roll." We finished our beers and exited the bar. Mike followed dutifully behind.

I led them through the house to my basement dungeon. My dungeon was fully outfitted.

"Take over, Leatherman." Steve stated.

Naturally dominant, I ordered the boy to strip, but to put his chaps and boots back on. He presented a nice package – nice pecs, muscular arms, and a virgin back and ass. The chaps framed his asscheeks, outlining the target for my flogger's destination.

Steve watched as I placed a Leather hood over Mike's head and shackled his boy with wrist and ankle restraints. I led him to my St. Andrew's cross. The boy stood silently as I locked him into place.

"You want to do the first rotation on your boy?" I asked Steve.

"Sir, you don't quite understand... I want you to work me over too."

Never one to miss an opportunity, I just happen to have extra gear for such an occasion. I ordered Steve to strip. He wore a Leather jock under his Leather pants. He was instructed to put his boots back on as I pulled out my second Leather hood. Naked except for his boots and jock, I handcuffed him to a support post which I often used as a flogging post.

Both boys stood silently as I readied my progression of floggers and whips.

I explained very quietly to each of them the number of rotations I would execute on their backs and asses.

My cock was getting harder as the first strip of Leather hit each of their backs.

Twenty-five from each of my six floggers, each one was progressively larger and more intense.

Between floggings, I would rub their reddening areas with my black Leather gloved hands. At first, I would tell them what to expect, but as the session lengthened and the floggings intensified, I said less and less to them.

Butt paddle. Riding crop. Cat o' nine tails with metal tips. Studded belt.

I'd occasionally reach around and feel their cocks. Both were reasonably hard.

I began the second rotation of floggings – numbered one through six. The build-up in intensity was beginning to make its 'mark' on their naked backs. Steve's back was reddening more quickly, but both stood stoically.

I applied alligators to both sets of nips. My own nips were already being tortured by my favorite nip-fuckers. The bulge in my pants felt great.

I lighted a cigar and blew smoke in each of their faces.

The assault continued for a long time. I actually lost track of time. I was thoroughly enjoying alternating between the two willing subjects.

My floggers continued to beat the ass and back of each subject. My cock was getting harder and harder in my cod. I rubbed it between floggings.

The boys stood obediently as we continued into the night. Fuck, I could continue all night.

I pulled a rubber dildo off my preparation table and after greasing it with some lube, inserted it in Steve's ass. "Keep it up there, son."

I positioned myself behind Mike, first rubbing my cod against his asscheeks. I was to have my way with the boy that I thought was hot, with the encouragement of his Master. Of course, his Master was still chained to the post and couldn't protest. I'd work on him later.

I spread Mike's ass cheeks with my gloved hands. I unsnapped my cod and my throbbing cock sprang forth. Lubed, my cock slid up his ass easily.

He began to moan as the cock climbed into his rectum.

Fuck. Felt great. I reached around and squeezed the alligators. He moaned and twisted. I began a slow rotation of pumping my cock in and out of his fuckhole.

My Leathered body was pressed against his naked body. Damn, my cock was pulsing inside this boy's ass as I continued to rub my new uniform against the boy's body.

The heavy Leather of my uniform rubbed against my already aroused body.

I was excited and so, I knew it wasn't going to be long before I shot a load up that handsome ass that I had admired only a couple of hours ago.

The boy was moaning more loudly as my cock increased its pumping action. I was like a fucking wild man as my cock exploded with a load of cum.

The boy's body shuddered as I shot. "Thank you, Sir," he whispered. He continued to shudder.

I picked up my flogger and began to assault his Master's ass. The dildo slid out and I shoved it back in. I flogged his ass even harder.

"Keep it in there, boy!" as I began slapping his ass with my butt paddle.

He squeezed his asscheeks tightly but to no avail, the dildo slid out again.

"I said keep it in there, boy, or you will pay the price..." Reinserted, it slid out once again as the next rotation began.

He shook his head 'No' and his body slumped forward in resignation to his fate.

Silently I unmanacled Mike and led him over, to stand directly behind his Master. His cock was full. I guided the boy's cock to his Master's hole. I lubed the boy's dick and motioned for him to shove his cock up his Master's hole.

He shook his head 'No' and trembled.

I held him by the neck and flogged his back.

"NOW!" I ordered. Not knowing what was going on, Steve flinched at my shouted command.

The boy obligingly stuck his cock's head near the asscheeks of the manacled Steve. I roughly squeezed the boy's cock and it responded by hardening. I spread Steve's asscheeks and guided the boy's dick into the fuckhole.

As the boy's dick grew, the boy began to enjoy the sensation of having his cock up his Master's hole. Steve responded by moaning and gyrating to the boy's grinding and pumping. The boy soon shot a load of cum. Steve slumped against the flogging pole after the load was delivered.

I unleashed Steve from his flogging position. Mike stood silently nearby, looking nervously in my direction.

Steve fell to his knees in front of me. "Thank you, Sir, that felt great." I unsnapped my cod and his willing mouth swallowed my cock and balls. They responded quickly and I shot a load down Steve's throat. As this was transpiring, I winked at the boy – it would be our little secret. Steve didn't seem to rationalize that it couldn't be me that shot two loads in his mouth and ass as well as up his boy's willing hole, in less than a few minutes. Okay, I'm good, but not that good.

Thus, my new uniform enjoyed its' maiden voyage. It had been broken in by not one, but two, willing boys. They have returned for several similar sessions and each time Mike has participated, with my guidance, in reversing the roles. Steve knows no different. Our little secret. Uniformly, a satisfying situation.

COME, MASTER CUM

The Leatherdaddy had a full day of work at the construction site. As was his custom, he wore his Leather codpieced pants, a white tee shirt, and his heavy metal-toed construction boots, spit-shined that morning by joe, his boy. When the Daddy returned, he was covered in sweat and mud. He didn't care – he had always been a hard worker and today was no exception. He sat down on the porch, just to rest a few minutes before his boy would return from his day's work.

The Daddy quickly fell into a deep slumber, his gloved hand absently massaging his piss-filled cock through the Leather cod.

When joe arrived home, his Master, his Leatherdaddy was asleep on the porch.

joe knew what to do. He shimmied his slender body under the chair in which his Daddy slept.

He began by licking the heels. Lifting the left foot gently, joe cleaned off the mud from the sole of the boot. He tongued it carefully, making sure there were no traces of mud. The toe, the sides of the sole, even the laces. He knew what his Daddy liked. Not a trace or mud, or joe would be punished. joe hoped he would be punished anyway. He enjoyed Daddy's whip and flogger.

When joe finished the first boot, he concentrated on the other. Leatherdaddy stirred in his sleep, but did not wake up. joe hoped he wouldn't until he had successfully finished Daddy's boots.

joe licked the other boot with enthusiasm and longing. He wanted Daddy's gloved hand to force his head down on the black Leather boot, but still the Daddy slept.

After a length of time joe finished the man's second boot and he looked longingly up into his Daddy's face. Eyes were tightly closed, snoring coming from his Master after what, joe surmised, was a long day at work. joe wanted his Leatherdaddy to be pleased with the results.

He began licking the pants which were tucked into the tops of the construction boots. The cod, he could see was packed with Daddy's handsome cock.

joe was tempted to unsnap and suck the manrod, but he knew that Daddy would not approve. Daddy gave the orders to unsnap his cod when he was ready to have his handsome cock serviced. The splotches of mud quickly disappeared from the pants as joe knelt before his Daddy. Each taste of mud and Leather brought him closer to the studded codpiece. The powerful aroma of mansweat, mud and Leather made joe's cock harden in his tight, faded blue jeans.

'Just one little peek...I've got to see Daddy's cock...' as joe unsnapped the left snap on the cod.

A gloved hand clamped down on joe's head.

'What did I tell you, boy, you know the fucking rules..." the Leatherdaddy growled.

"I'm sorry, Sir, I just couldn't resist your handsome cock," sputtered joe.

"We've gone over this before, boy, you KNOW THE RULES."

"I'm sorry, Sir, forgive me, Sir, I just worship you and your..." the boy pleaded.

The Daddy ordered joe to kneel before him, hands behind his back, all the while massaging his cock within his codpiece.

"Even though you did a good job on my boots, bootlicker, If a boy doesn't obey his Master, he must be punished."

"Yes, Sir."

The Daddy pulled joe's body toward him and thrust his tongue in the boy's mouth.

"Yes, Daddy. I will take your punishment," joe attempted to say as the tongue explored joe's willing mouth.

Daddy's muscled arms encircled the boy's frame, caressing the boy's denim-covered asscheeks. The Daddy began a slow paddling with his left glove-covered hand. The spanking felt delicious after a long day at work and joe's cock arched upward in its denim enclosure. Soon, the boy's crotch was resting against the crotch of his seated Daddy. The Daddy and boy were intertwined, man – and boy – sweat and the powerful aroma of Leather, intermingling. The boy's cock was throbbing from the intimate contact of it resting so near to the Daddy's cod. The boy's chest pressed against the sweat-soaked tee shirt of his Dad.

The Leatherdaddy knew that the boy was coming close to jacking off as he abruptly pushed the boy away.

"No, Daddy, don't stop..." the boy pleaded.

"Enough, boy, I told you, you had to be punished... now, I want you to control your cock, don't you jack or you will be punished."

The boy squeezed his eyes shut, and tried to think of anything but his Daddy's masculine body. It did little good. Within seconds, a wet stain appeared on the jeans.

"You little fuck up..." the Daddy growled as he grabbed the boy's crotch. His vicelike grip clenched the head of the boy's penis through the denim. That action made joe's cock shoot an even bigger load of cum.

joe was led to the workover room. His Daddy removed joe's clothing and joe was placed spread-eagle on the table. His feet and arms were placed in restraints and his cock and balls were placed in a Leather pouch. A strap was tightly buckled around the top of the pouch and a lock secured it in place. joe's cock and balls were prisoners in a Leather prison – a chastity bag. A chain was attached from the strap to a hook in the ceiling and soon joe's cock and balls were being pulled upward to a point of discomfort.

"Stay like that for a while, boy."

If joe moved from side to side, the balls and cock were pulled into an even more uncomfortable position. His only choice was to lie as Daddy had placed him. The Daddy lighted a big cigar and took several long draws on it while deliberately looking over his paddles hanging neatly on the wall. He finally selected a pinprick paddle. He began to methodically tenderize his boy's flesh, chest, legs, inner thighs, and the reachable portions of asscheeks. Daddy and boy had been through this before – it was one of joe's favorites activities and despite his mental attempt to stay soft, his cock responded to the delicious treatment. It was obvious that the Daddy's cock had responded too, a noticeable bulge in his codpiece attested to that.

A pair of murderous titclamps bit into the boy's titflesh, placed there by his Daddy's gloved hands. joe normally relished the feeling, but this action only made his cock harder and more uncomfortable. joe's cock arched upward in the Leather bag.

Next, Daddy inserted a slender dildo into the boy's hole. That momentarily softened the boy's erection, but joe's mind instinctively recognized it as the one Daddy favored and his cock hardened once again.

The Leatherdaddy took off his rough work gloves and placed his buttery soft black Leather gloves on.

"Oh, no," joe inwardly moaned, "not those..."

Daddy knew what he was doing and began rubbing the boy's naked body with the soft gloves. In long caressing motions, the gloves stroked the boy's shoulders, arms, down the rib cage, hips, and thighs. The Daddy concentrated on rubbing the boy's ribcage area, because he knew the boy especially enjoyed it and it would make his cock even more uncomfortable.

The Daddy had a knowing smile on his face. The boy's cock was pulsing within the Leather bag.

"Don't you shoot on my Leathers, boy... your ass is history if you do..."

"Daddy," the boy begged, "it is so hard not to shoot... I'm trying..."

The Daddy rubbed the boy's body in even longer strokes, terminating the rubdown with a swat at the asscheeks.

The boy's cock pulsated in the Leather bag.

The Leatherman pulled a Leather hood off the shelf and laced it tightly into place on his boy's head. The boy's eyes peered nervously out of the eyeholes, but the mouth portion was soon filled with a pecker gag – the boy was unable to speak.

The Daddy reached his gloved hands to the Leather pouch containing the boy's cock and balls. The cock was hardened and pulsating. The Leatherman knew that all he had to do was touch it and the boy's cock would explode.

The boy was pleading with his eyes and shaking his head yes.

The Leatherdaddy stood poised for what seemed an eternity. The boy anticipated the manly squeeze of his Daddy's hands.

"Not yet, cocksucker," the Daddy warned as he squeezed the bag gently, "Not yet."

The boy thought, "Please, Daddy, soon... I can't control it. Please let me shoot, Daddy..."

The Daddy slapped the pouch with his gloved hand. The boy's cock throbbed as did the Daddy's.

The Daddy reached underneath the pouch and squeezed the boy's balls, pinching them through the Leather.

"No, Daddy, please don't do that," the boy thought, attempting to send the message telepathically.

His balls were aching with the fullness of the tightened pouch around their base.

The Leatherdaddy continued to pinch the balls through the Leathers and rubbing his other gloved hand on the pouch where the head of joe's cock was straining against the pouch.

The boy started twisting from side to side, pulling his balls and cock even harder – they were stretched above his body and were throbbing and aching from the strain on them. He knew he would shoot soon – even if Daddy didn't tell him to.

The Daddy only increased the pressure, now encircling the base of the boy's cock and balls with his gloved hand. He squeezed harder and harder and the boy's cock throbbed with an intensity that he had never felt before.

With his other black gloved Leather hand, the man rolled the tight balls between his fingers and the palm of his hand.

"Daddy, pleeease... release them...." the boy thought, as he writhed from side to side. His cock felt like it would break out through the thick Leather pouch.

"Don't you shoot, you cocksucker... that's an order," the Leatherdaddy growled as he increased the pressure around the base of the boy's cock and balls. Of course, talking about it only intensifying joe's urge to shoot a load even with the vicelike grip.

After what seemed an eternity, the Leatherdaddy abruptly loosened his grip, pulled the chain down from the ceiling and held the boy's cock and ball bag in his gloved hands. He climbed on top of the table, laid squarely on top of the boy, and ordered, "SHOOT!"

The boy's cock released a geyser of cum in the little Leather pouch. It kept coming and coming. joe's body shuddered from the sheer force of the ejaculation He could feel his cock and balls enveloped in a thick layer of cum. The boy was heaving from relief.

The Daddy's cock sprang forth from the Daddy's cod as the Daddy unsnapped his own cod. His cock was throbbing with an intensity too. The Leatherman's cum shot a geyser of mancum all over his boy's chest and hips. The man lifted his boy's head, removed the pecker gag, and thrust his tongue into the cigar hole.

Man and boy remained in that position for some time, until the cum had dried on the boy's belly and within his cock's recently-found Leather enclosure. When he was finally released, joe was told to lay on the floor on the workover room. The chastity bag was taken off his cock and balls and joe, the bootlicker, was ordered to clean the insides of the bag. When the bag was cleaned to Daddy's specifications, it was placed with the other toys. It was no longer a new toy – it had been christened with the spent efforts of Daddy's boy. The Leatherdaddy was a good Master, always introducing new toys for the mutual enjoyment of both man and boy. joe's punishment was at once torture and a delicious reward. joe would do anything to please his Daddy. He would gladly change his name to cumlicker. joe hoped the next time, however, the chastity bag would enclose Daddy's cock and balls and the cum would be his Master's.

A Boner Book

BOYCOP

The Leatherman had experienced a rough week of work, and as Friday waned, he couldn't wait to get to his Leather lair and shed his white collar shit suit and tie, trading them in for his soft, buttery, ass-tight Leathers.

The commute home was just as horrible with a bunch of morons and assholes cutting in and out of traffic, eliciting several epithets from the otherwise calm man. Finally, after an excruciatingly long forty five minutes, he pulled into his driveway, retrieved his mail, and entered his Leather refuge from the world. He threw off the suit and tie, discarded on the floor, and reached for his Leathers. Only after that did he bother to check the pile of mail with the usual credit card applications, bills, and useless shit. Then he checked telephone messages and finally his email. Most of it was spam, but his eyes were attracted to the flashing red exclamation point next to an email from 'boycop'.

Not knowing who this was, he wasn't sure he wanted to open it, for fear it might spread a computer virus. Still, 'boycop' intrigued him and so, when he opened it, he read the following:

Daddy, I'm your boy and a cop. Let's meet in the woods and you can shove your nightstick up my ass..." The Leatherdaddy was a cautious man and so, he simply deleted the message without replying. As the midnight hour approached, the Leatherman had forgotten the week as his comfortable Leathers caressed his masculine body. With a cigar clenched between his teeth and a few toys attached to his belt for pleasuring himself, he was ready for a long walk in the woods. His boy carl was visiting his college roommate this weekend and so, the man was headed out for some self-abuse. As he exited his house, he viewed a cloudless night with a full moon and stars gracing the sky. The woods was an isolated spot, known only to the Leatherman. It was on a corner of his property. To access the woods, the Leatherman had to cross a busy four lane highway which had cut through the property years before the Leatherman owned it. As the speed limit was reduced from 50 mph to just 25 mph, cops often sat in a cul-de-sac and issued speeding tickets when they needed to reach their quota. The Leatherman knew all five cops who comprised the local Police Department, none of whom he wished to fuck. Uniformly, they were men with big egos, bellies that hung over their belts, and as intimidating to the Leatherman as someone's grandmother. Sooner or later, all five had stopped the Leatherman in his walks to 'interrogate' him. He had treated them with respect and they had 'let him go' with warning that they would be watching him. 'Big fucking deal' he growled under his breath on each occasion as he continued his marches.

As he approached the road, he stood watching the heavy volume of traffic before proceeding across the highway. As he reached the shoulder on the other side of the road, a pair of headlights caught him in their beams like a deer. A spot flashlight was soon trained right in his eyes.

A voice from the patrol car announced, "Stay right there, don't move."

The Leatherman obliged, dragging on his cigar as the cop got out of the vehicle and cautiously approached him.

"Let me see your hands above your head..."

The Leatherman raised his arms in compliance.

A young fellow in cop's uniform approached him, but it wasn't one of the regulars. This guy was new and decidedly more handsome than the others. It was apparent that he was attempting to exert his authority, but the Leatherman wasn't even mildly intimidated.

"Sir, it has been reported that there is drug activity in this vicinity and I am here to investigate. I am Trooper Vincent, on temporary reassignment from the state. May I see some identification?"

"I don't have any on me – the property on either side of the road is mine and I don't feel it necessary for me to carry that with me."

"And what is your name, Sir?"

The Leatherman told him.

"Remain where you are, Sir, while I confirm that information." With that the patrolman returned to his vehicle, hidden by an outcropping of bushes.

The Leatherman approached the cop's car, alarming the patrolman.

He drew his gun from his holster and said, "I told you to remain where you are, Sir".

"Look, Buddy, I told you who I am and you're beginning to irritate me..." With that the Leatherman stood with his legs against the door of the cop car and his bulging codpiece resting on the frame of the open window. He blew a column of smoke into the cop's car.

The cop gulped as a report came over the car's radio, confirming that the Leatherman was indeed the owner of the property.

"No disrespect intended. I am merely doing my job, Sir." With that the young cop placed the gun back in his holster and returned the radio to its cradle.

"It's all right, son, I know you're just doing your job, and I intend to do my job, boycop."

"Whaat?" the cop answered, as his head jerked upward, catching the gaze of the Leatherman.

"I got your email this afternoon, boy."

"Sir, I don't know what you are talking about, I am an officer of the law."

"It would seem to me, son, that since you are parked on my property that you will obey the laws of the Leatherman."

"Excuse me, Sir?" as the young cop started to pick up the radio, to dispatch a distress signal.

"PUT THE FUCKING RADIO DOWN AND GET OUT OF THE FUCKING CAR, NOW!"

In his head-to-toe Leathers, black Leather gloves, and knee-high Dehner boots, the Leatherman was an intimidating presence and the young cop exited the car.

"Now, Sir, I have to inform you that you have..." The boy didn't immediately realize that the Leatherman wasn't paying any attention to the rhetoric, instead he was taking a good look at the young cop. He was about twenty five with a military crew cut and the athletic body required for a Leatherboy. His blue uniform hugged the young boy's frame. The boy's trousers were neatly creased and tucked into the tops of military, laced boots. The Leatherman could see that the cop was nervous. The cop continued his rehearsed banter until the Leatherman yelled, "SHUT THE FUCK UP, BOY."

The boy obliged momentarily and before he knew what was happening, the Leatherman had handcuffed his hands behind his back.

The two marched into the woods, the Leatherman holding onto the boy's cuffed hands with an iron grip with one Leathered hand, the other clamped tightly over the boy's mouth. The boy struggled occasionally, but it did little good. The Leatherman's strength intensified when he knew there was a potential Leatherboy to work over and after all, it had been a shitty week.

They marched for a good ten minutes before coming to a clearing, cleared by the Leatherman himself. A fallen tree proved the perfect place to position the boy against it, his hands now manacled behind the tree.

The boy struggled but could not extricate himself from the cuffs or the tree.

"Relax, boy, you're going to experience my form of interrogation." With that he fondled the boy's crotch.

"Sir, I am an officer of the law and this is a state offense..."

The boy's hardened cock in his pants contradicted what the boy had just stated.

"Yeah, okay, boy, you can arrest me when it's over..."

The Leatherman unbuckled the boy's pants, unzipped the zipper, only to reveal a Leather jockstrap bulging with the boy's nine inches.

"Well..." the Leatherman chuckled, "what would your commander say about this? Is this a state-issued jock?"

Revealed, the boy could only answer, "Please, Sir, I can explain, I did email you... it was me. I had heard about you at the headquarters and just had to see for myself..."

"I know, Son. I could tell you were boycop the minute I saw you. You're a cut above the rest of the department. You're very handsome," the Leatherman said as he squeezed the boy's loaded jock, "and from what I can tell, you have got a really nice dick. Let Daddy judge for himself."

With the compliments at hand, the boy began to relax.

The Leatherman pulled the jock down, releasing the boy's cock. The Leatherdaddy pulled a small cock whip off his belt and began to beat the boy's cock and balls gently. The boy began moaning as his cock responded to the expert treatment inflicted by his new Leatherdaddy.

"Don't you cum until I tell you, boy."

"Yes, Sir," the boy moaned, but he couldn't control his cock juices and they soon exploded, landing on the Daddy's Leather-covered thigh.

The Leatherdaddy slapped the boy across the face with his Leather-gloved hand. He wiped the cum off with a red bandana he carried in his back pocket.

"I'm sorry, Sir..." the boy began to apologize as the cum-soaked bandana was shoved in his mouth. The Daddy removed the handcuffs long enough to remove the boy's uniform shirt. It revealed a firmly muscled chest.

The Daddy repositioned the boy so that he was facing the tree trunk. His pants were pulled down around his knees.

"As your judge, boy, I hereby sentence you to twenty lashings with my cat o'nine tails flogger." The flogger was a mean little fucker with metal tips at the end of each Leather strap. Twenty lashings on the boy's back were followed by twenty lashings on the boy's sweet ass.

The boy did not resist. He was mumbling something.

The Leatherman took the gag out and demanded to know what the boy was saying.

"Thank you, Daddy, please I deserve more..."

The Daddy was glad to find such a willing boy and gave him twenty more of each.

With that the Daddy pulled out a small tube of lube and greased up his right Leathered fist.

"You got any drugs, boy?" as he shoved his Leathered fist up the boy's hole.

The boy's scream abruptly stopped as the Daddy shoved the rag back in the boy's mouth.

The man worked the boy's hole over for some time as his own cock hardened in his codpiece.

Eventually, the man removed his fist. He repositioned the boy, shoving him roughly down on his knees. With the cuffs back in place, he ordered the boy to suck his Daddy's cock. The Daddy removed the bandana from the young cop's mouth.

The Leatherman unsnapped his codpiece and his own manrod sprang forth.

The boy swallowed the man's cock without hesitation.

The Daddy pounded his manflesh into the boy's willing mouth and within minutes had shot a load which squirted out of the boy's mouth onto the boy's chin. The boy willingly lapped up every drop.

The Leatherdaddy pushed the boy's head backward and played with his own mancock for several minutes. The boy continued to lick his lips, making sure he had gotten every droplet of man juice.

The Daddy shoved the bandana back into the boy's mouth, repositioned the boy once again so that he was facing the tree, and began to leave. The boy shook his head 'No', but the Daddy left anyway.

When the Daddy returned about twenty minutes later, the boy was attempting to pull the handcuffs off his wrists. The Daddy just laughed at the endeavor and watched the boy's vain attempts for a few minutes before revealing himself.

The boy turned his head expectantly as the Daddy marched into the clearing, the boy's own nightstick in his hand.

Session Two was about to begin as the nightstick received a layering of lube.

"Bend over, boy."

The night was young, the moon was full, and once the night was over, 'interrogation' had a whole new meaning to a young cop, reassigned to the local police department permanently at his own request.

REWARD:
REVENGE & A BOX OF CUBANS

The plan for revenge began on Friday afternoon – about fifteen minutes after I was called into the CEO's office. I was told that my services were no longer needed and I had fifteen minutes to clear out my personal belongings from the office I had occupied for the last fifteen years. I was escorted to my office and out to the parking lot by an associate who had his nose so far up the CEO's butt, you could no longer see his face. I wouldn't give him the satisfaction of shaking his proffered hand, wishing me 'good luck' in my new ventures. 'Fuck you, you asshole' is what I countered with.

What they didn't know is that they had now given me plenty of time to plot revenge.

After all, I am a Leatherman. I am a sadist. I am used to whipping boys, fisting their asses, and making them beg for mercy.

I laid low for a month, collecting unemployment and gathering needed information.

Six weeks to the day – darkness fell and the Leatherman in full black Leather began my three and a half mile march to the CEO's private club. I took backroads and shortcuts so that I was unobserved by anyone. The necessary gear was strapped to my belt.

The CEO tended to linger at his club after a very messy divorce (when we heard about the divorce, many of us hoped that she had financially castrated him) among his cronies, with lots of drinks and elicit Cuban cigars.

I located his Mercedes on the parking lot and as I suspected, it was unlocked. I crawled into the back and hunkered down. I placed my executioner's hood over my face and waited.

I waited patiently, going over my plan.

My ears were alerted to the crunch of gravel and the jingling of his keys. He seated himself in the car and he started the ignition. As he pulled on his shoulder belt, I swiftly caught his left hand with my left hand and my other gloved hand went over his mouth and nostrils. I shoved a pecker gag hard into his mouth and with my free hand, now caught his other hand before he was able to blow the horn of the car. He struggled but frankly was no match for me. I worked out at the YMCA four days a week, he went to his private spa once a week. With his two wrists gripped firmly in my left hand, I slipped a readied rope over the wrists and pulled tight. I then quickly wrapped the roping around his arms.

My roping techniques with struggling boys came in very handy on this occasion.

The pecker gag was buckled into place – no possibility that he could scream. Moving him to the backseat proved more of a challenge. With my booted foot, I kicked the back door open and before he had a chance to react, yanked the driver's door open, dragging him out onto the gravel. He kicked and struggled. I gave him a gut punch which momentarily knocked the wind out of him. It gave me enough time to hoist him onto the back seat and binding his feet with a prepared second piece of rope. Aah, bondage rope! A sadistic Leatherman's best friend! I added a black bandana over his eyes as a blindfold.

I pushed him down on the floor of the car just as two men exited the club. I hastily jumped into the driver's seat and pulled out of the parking lot before they had a chance to view which car was leaving.

As we drove to my place, I watched him in the rear-view mirror as he struggled against the bondage ropes. I could have told him that I'm an excellent ropesman. There was no possibility of escape.

I pulled the car into my driveway and dragged his sorry ass out of the backseat. He continued to struggle as I forced him down the basement steps into my private dungeon. As a precaution against unruly boys, I had soundproofed the dungeon.

I pushed him down the last step as he resisted me strenuously. He fell down the last step – his hobbled feet getting in the way. I kicked him twice, just to show him who was now boss. It also alerted him to the fact that the bossman's steel-toed boots could hurt. The fall seemed to stun him and I took advantage of it. I momentarily released his hands from bondage as I ripped off his perfectly-tied bow tie (he wore one every day) and tore at his shirt (the one with his initials carefully embroidered on the cuff). I would take special delight in pissing on both of them.

I rolled him easily on the bondage table, where his wrists were now manacled to the sides of the table. This action seemed to renew his resistance and he flailed his arms, pulling at the restraints.

"Go ahead, fucker, try... they're steel," I growled, "Wear yourself down. Less resistance to the nights ahead."

He attempted to kick me with his hobbled feet. I removed his expensive loafers and discarded them.

Pressing down on one leg at a time, I eventually got his trousers off only to discover his Calvin Kleins. A knife cinched to my waistband cut through the elastic. Another potential jack rag was instantly made...

His cock was shrunken up – frightened, I suppose. With good reason.

Finally, my flogging subject was spread-eagled and naked on the bondage table. To add some additional 'security' – the same ropes that had made him my captive now trussed him in place so that he could not squirm too much.

I once again growled, "You are now my prisoner. You will come to find out and admit that you are a worthless piece of shit. No one cares that you have disappeared." He began trembling, shaking his head from side to side. I remedied that by placing a block of wood on either side of his head, minimalizing movement.

With that, the torture of my subject began.

I placed manfucking nipple clamps on his virgin tits His shrunken cock and balls were placed in a pinprick chastity ball bag. A dildo was shoved up his ass and secured. Don't feel sorry for him – he was a real bastard. Over the years that he had been CEO, he had let people go right before they were eligible for retirement, relieving them of their potential benefits. A buddy of mine had been injured on the job and had been granted medical leave. The day after he returned to work, he was let go on trumped up charges. I considered calling them and letting them take a few licks at him. No, this fucker was all mine.

I began flogging his chest, making sure I caught the chain of the nip clamps with the flogger, pulling on his tits. His shoulders got a healthy dose of the flogger too.

Hell, this was fun. I lighted up one of his expensive Cubans from the cigar pouch from his shirt pocket. It tasted pretty damned good.

Moving to the head of the table, I removed the blindfold and the pecker gag. As predicted, he began screaming.

"Scream all you want, bitch," I snarled.

I blew the smoke from his expensive Cuban right in his face. I spit in his face too. His screams were quickly subdued as I placed a full bondage hood over his face. I unzipped the mouth area, but without any forethought, jammed his bowtie into his mouth. It was an executive decision. It was an executioner's decision too.

"Go ahead and scream... choke if you want to."

I exited the dungeon and drove his car into my garage. It must have been my lucky day – a whole box of unopened Cubans were on the passenger's seat.

I returned to the dungeon and all was quiet. The boy was laying prone and I momentarily worried that he had choked. I removed the bowtie only to find that he was breathing normally. He apparently was dozing, effects perhaps of all the alcohol he had consumed that evening. Let the fucker sleep.

I retired to my bed and slept soundly.

I woke early, and found the boy in a deeper sleep.

Without waking him, I maneuvered him onto his stomach and manacled him to the four corners of the bondage table. He'd wake soon enough as I pulled my flogger off the wall of toys. With the second strike, he woke. His head raised and his arms and legs strained against the restraints. A healthy scream ripped through the dungeon. Time to put the pecker gag back in his mouth.

With that, I let loose a barrage of paddlings and floggings. My anger at the way I was treated boiled over. His ass and back were marked with my flogging patterns. I hoped they would remain for some time.

"You worthless cocksucking piece of shit." I yelled. Not fully awake, I assume he didn't recognize my voice.

"You can stay here forever." I left the dungeon to calm down. I have never taken my full fury out on a boy like I had just done. I'm a sadist, and a Leatherman, and proud of it, but I do respect a boy's limits and have treated them with human respect. I rationalized that this asshole had ruined so many lives, metaphorically fucking them in the ass.

The more I thought about it, the angrier I got. I went back downstairs and beat him some more.

I kept him in total bondage for three days, although I got him up to give him water, feed him, and escorted him to the bathroom. I hovered over him with a bullwhip just in case he tried to escape. Each time, I wore my hood so that he wouldn't recognize me. I took special delight in filling his hole with a different, and larger, dildo each day. On several occasions, I couldn't resist the temptation, climbing on to the table and jamming my excited cock up his ass.

I lost track of how many flogging sessions we had. During the time, my anger at him solidified.

On the fourth day, a news report appeared on the television concerning the CEO's disappearance. The ass-sniffer that had escorted me to the parking lot was interviewed – he looked extremely nervous, wiping sweat off of his forehead as he spoke.

On the morning of the fifth day, the television reporters indicated that federal agents had confiscated the CEO's computer and financial records. It was now assumed that the CEO had fled the country – a large amount of money was unaccounted for. Suddenly, the asshole sniffer was under indictment and a warrant for the arrest of the CEO had been issued.

My sadistic mind started turning, formulating yet another plan. I woke early on the next morning – the prisoner was snoring soundly. I carefully unmanacled him, putting his rumpled shirt and trousers back on him. The flogging marks were not visible, of course. I carefully retied his bowtie. I placed him back in bondage. I tore off a piece of a sadist's second product of choice – duct tape. The duct tape went over his mouth I then bound his ankles and wrists, leaving the roll of tape hanging from his wrists. He woke in the middle of all this, but didn't put up much resistance. I guess I had finally broken his spirit.

After darkness fell, I loaded him into his Mercedes and drove to the State Police Barracks.

I positioned him in the driver's seat and took particular delight in ripping the tape off his mouth.

"Now scream, you worthless bag of shit," I yelled. He just looked at my hooded face without expression. No spark of recognition when we made eye contact for the briefest of seconds.

I hastily exited, disappearing into the night. It took me almost three hours to walk back to my dungeon.

It's been two years since I made a deposit at the Police Barracks. I'm pleased to say that CEO stands for Convicted of Embezzling Offenses. Okay, I made that up. He was put away for a long time as was his assistant. The company was restructured and in a strange twist of fate (not even I would believe this is how the story ended), I was hired as the new CEO. In quick order, I have rehired all those who were badly treated.

No one quite believes the former CEO's outrageous stories of kidnap and torture – he apparently never realized who his kidnapper and torturer was. The public at large thought that he probably put duct tape around his ankles and hands to garner sympathy. And I'm certain that he hasn't shared too many of the stories in prison, lest his hole be stretched more than it was.

As I finish writing this, I'm lighting up a Cuban cigar. It's from my private stock – a gift from a boy who never bothered to say 'Thank you, Sir'. Guess I'll just have to beat his ass again, in ten to twenty years.

FOUND IN THE WOODS

The Leatherman glided off onto the side of the road and killed the motor to his Harley. An urgency to take a piss had prompted this action.

He marched into the underbrush of the woods and found a sturdy tree against which to relieve himself. He unsnapped his studded codpiece and his manhood burst forth, full of manpiss. A nicely-veined shaft with a mushroom head sprang forth. The man admired his cock and fondled it for several minutes. As he continued to fondle his cock, he sensed that he was not alone and as he scanned the landscape, he saw a slight movement, a change in shadows, behind a nearby tree.

He pushed his cock back in his cod and resnapped the codpiece. He marched toward the shadow.

He viewed a blonde beauty, perhaps twenty-five or so. The boy was lost in his own jack-off reverie. It gave the Daddy a chance to view the boy. He wore a tight white tee shirt, with nice looking pecs filling the shirt out nicely. Faded blue jeans caressed the boy's thighs with a tightness that promised a firm ass. The boy had both hands wrapped firmly around his lengthy, slender cock. The boy had his eyes closed and he moaned softly as he stroked his meat slowly and deliberately.

The Daddy's cock was already throbbing as he marched closer to the boy and wrapped his own gloved hands around the boy's hands.

The boy's eyes flew open and his mouth emitted an "Ohhh" before the Daddy's mouth closed over the surprised boy's mouth.

He kissed the boy's mouth long and hard before his tongue began exploring the inner recesses of the boy's willing mouth. His hands squeezed the boy's hands as he felt the boy shoot a load onto the Daddy's gloved hands. The Daddy smeared his cum-stained gloved hands on the boy's cheeks before grabbing them and pulling the boy's face closer to his own.

They kissed for a long time.

The Daddy's cock was hard and throbbing inside his cod.

"You take piss, boy?"

"No...mister... I was just playing..."

"Well, son, you do now."

He forced the boy down on his knees, but the boy struggled to get away.

He was no match for the Leatherman, who thrust his cod into the boy's face.

The boy's eyes were transfixed on the man's mound.

"When a Leatherdaddy tells you to do something, boy, you do it... no questioning."

"No, sir, really..." as the boy shook his head.

The Daddy unsnapped his cod and his manrod slapped the boy on the cheek. He guided his cock into the boy's mouth which he forced open with his powerful, gloved hands.

The Leatherman's cock fully filled the boy's mouth and the boy had no option but to swallow it as best he could.

A steady flow of manpiss now filled the boy's mouth. The pissing seemed to go on forever.

The boy's demeanor changed as he began to gulp greedily until the last drops of piss exited the man's piss slit.

"Now, suck me, boy." the Leatherdaddy commanded.

The boy complied more readily and began to lubricate the shaft with his tongue.

"Good, boy" as the man pushed the boy's head toward his substantial bull balls. The boy's eyes caught the Leatherman's eyes as a brief smile was seen on the boy's face.

"Thank you, Sir," the boy mumbled as he continued to suck the man's rod and lick his heavy balls.

"You're welcome, boy."

The sucking continued until the man's shaft was fully engorged with cum. After a time, he shot a load down the boy's throat.

"Thank you, Sir," the boy repeated as he continued to tongue the cum off his newly-found Daddy's cock.

Finally, the man pushed the boy's head away.

"Lie face down, boy."

"Why?" the boy questioned. With one motion, the Leatherman ripped the boy's tee shirt off the boy's body.

"A boy doesn't question his Leatherman, boy, now just do it."

The boy lay down on the leaves that carpeted the floor of the wooded area.

The man knelt between the boy's legs which he spread apart. He reached underneath and unbuttoned the boy's jeans. He pulled them down the boy's legs and threw them to one side. The boy's sneakers were discarded as well.

He began rubbing the boy's asscheeks with his gloved hands. He reached into his motorcycle jacket pocket, retrieving a small tube of lubricant.

He rubbed it generously on his right gloved hand.

The boy began struggling, as he knew what was coming next.

Before he could issue a protest, however, the Leatherman's fist was up the boy's virgin ass. The man covered the boy's mouth with a gloved hand as the boy began to scream.

"I'm popping your fucking cherry, boy, and there ain't nothing you can do about it."

The boy struggled more violently but by this time, the man had the boy's legs pinned down.

The boy could only lie helplessly and endure the fisting.

The man's fist explored the boy's hole for a long, sensuous time.

The Leatherman's cock was erect, this time with a cockload of cum.

After what seemed an eternity to the boy, the Leatherman removed his fist. The boy was sweating profusely and was breathing heavily.

The Leatherdaddy pulled out his cock and juiced it up with the Leathered glove.

Without warning once again, the Leatherman thrust his cock up the lubed-up hole.

"Take it like the boy you are, son," as the Leatherdaddy penetrated the boy's fuckhole.

The Leatherman pulled the cock in and out of the boy's hole, each time it seemed to reach a little further up the boy's ass.

The boy moaned as he was being raped by the big, sturdy Leatherman. The Leatherman eased himself down upon the body of the boy, his cock arched upward into the rectum.

The man began rubbing the boy's arms and hands with his tight, black Leather gloves. His big mantits pressed against the boy's back. He had spread his cycle jacket so it encased both man and boy. His muscular Leathered thighs rubbed against the back of the boy's legs.

"This is what it feels like to be with a real Leatherman. I assume you like it?"

The boy could only shake his head as the pounding of the mancock and the Leather rubdown continued.

The Leatherman thought no more about the boy's displeasure or pleasure, but concentrated on his own. His cock was fully engorged with cockcum.

After a period, the Leatherman cranked the thrusting up a notch and began a frenzied pounding into the boy's hole. The boy was a good receptacle for his cockfuck and he was going to enjoy it to the maximum.

The man's head arched upward as he reached that point of climax.

With one mighty thrust, he shot a load which lubricated the boy's hole. The Leatherdaddy let out a triumphant yell as the boy screamed. Cum seeped out of the boy's hole.

The Daddy pulled his cock out of the boy's hole. He flipped the boy over and sat on the boy's chest.

"Lick it clean, boy," the Leatherdaddy ordered as threads of cum dripped out of the piss-slit.

After the boy had cleaned the man's cock, he lay on his back, naked and panting. His chest was heaving.

Without warning, the Leatherman spread-eagled himself on top of the boy. His muscular frame covered the boy and soon the man was molesting the boy with his powerful gloved hands and substantial Leathered frame, pulling on the boy's tits, slapping his naked body, spitting in the boy's face, and cursing him for being so inexperienced..

The boy responded to this activity with more enthusiasm and soon was clinging to the Leatherdaddy.

"Please, Sir, I want to be your fuckboy... I want this every day."

The boy's face looked shocked when the Leatherman slapped him across the face. "I make that determination, boy, if you are worthy of being my fuckboy."

The Leatherman stood up and kicked the boy's ass with his booted foot.

"I'm sorry, Sir, I didn't mean..."

"Shut up," the Leatherman growled as he stuck the toe of his boot in the center of the boy's chest.

"Lick my boot, boy." The boy tongued the boot as best he could while he lay prone on the ground underneath the boot.

"Not good enough, boy, do it again."

The boy continued to lick every seam of the boot as best he could. His hands grasped the boot as he drew it toward his slave mouth. The Daddy stood watching every move, pressing the boot into the boy's mouth when he thought the boy had missed a section.

He reached in his motorcycle jacket and pulled out a cigar case. Unwrapping it and clipping it, he began to suck on a dick-sized cigar while the tonguing continued.

Once satisfied that his right boot was clean, the Leatherman shifted feet and the boy was soon licking the left boot.

Finally, the boots had been tongued to the Leatherman's satisfaction.

"Get up, boy." The boy stood up, his head lowered, his hands by his side.

"Put your clothes on, boy." The boy obeyed and they were soon marching toward the Harley. "Get on, boy."

The Daddy mounted the Harley and the boy crawled on behind him.

"What's your name, boy?"

"George, Sir, but I hope you will call me Leatherboy, Sir."

"You'll do for now, Leatherboy." The Daddy flatly stated.

They sped along the country roads leading them away from their point of encounter.

The boy's torn tee shirt flapped in the wind. The boy pressed his firm chest against the Daddy's Leather jacket.

A cock bulge in the boy's jeans pressed against the man's Leathered ass. The boy inched his hands up toward the man's pecs and began massaging his Daddy's mantits.

The man's cock rose in his codpiece. The boy knew he was having an effect on the man's cockmound and unsnapped the left side of the cod. He reached in and slowly rubbed the shaft of his Daddy's cock. The cock grew harder and harder as they proceeded down the highway. The boy rubbed the cockshaft harder and harder, fingering the piss slit each time he reached the top of the shaft.

"Damn, what a good boy," thought the Leatherman as he arched his back and shot a load into the willing boy's hand.

The boy greedily licked the cum off his hand as the cycle carried them to the Leatherman's lair and for an afternoon of flogging and whipping.

The boy had passed Session I with flying colors. Would he do as well in Session II?

THE LAUNDROMAT

This story is dedicated to Christopher.

It had been a shitty week at work. The construction supervisor had warned me twice that my appearance needed cleaning up. My tee shirt was soaked with mansweat and my jeans and boots were crusty with mud. Hell, it was a construction site, but this guy was a stickler for appearance. "Have 'em cleaned up by Monday or you're out of a job," he warned me as I left Friday afternoon.

"Shit," I thought, "he gets good work out of me and I'm supposed to look like a fuckin' preppy when I come to work..."

I couldn't afford to lose the job, my mortgage and my other bills were due at the end of the following week. I gathered up the crusty jeans and tee shirts, discarding all the shit that accumulated in the pockets, heaping it on the bed to be sorted later. Going down to the basement, I put a load in my washer, only to find that it wouldn't work. I tinkered with the damned thing for an hour and a half before realizing that two belts, not just one, had split and needed replacement. In the interests of time, I loaded the socks, tees, and jeans in the saddlebag of my cycle. The only pants I had left were a pair of jean shorts and it was frigging cold outside. I put my Leather chaps over them, threw on my cycle jacket, and headed to the local laundromat.

I hastily threw my clothes in a washer and as I reached for my wallet, it wasn't there. I'd left it on the bed when I had thrown the crusty jeans into the wash.

"Shit," I thought.

At that point, a young fellow was loading his laundry into a machine several washers away.

"Hey, Buddy," I asked, "do you think you could spare a cup of detergent and a $1.25 in quarters? I left my wallet at home."

The guy looked startled at my request. He was young, hair falling over his eyes, a rim beard. He was wearing knee-high Wescos, black jeans, and a Leather jacket which would pass for a cycle jacket. A rubber tee enhanced his boyish torso.

"Sure, Sir." as he handed me the box of detergent. He reached into his tight jeans and extracted a handful of quarters. I picked them out of his hand, first eyeing the nice tight basket in his jeans, and then made sure I made eye-contact when I thanked him.

He kept his head lowered as we both started our machines.

"You from around here, Buddy?"

"No... Sir."

"My buddies call me G.W.," as I stuck out my hand in greeting.

"Glad to meet you, Sir," as the boy tentatively shook my hand.

"Can I repay your kindness by offering you a cigar?" I asked. My cigar pouch was in my cycle jacket. I pulled it out and offered him a Montecristo Churchill.

The boy took it and nodded his head in thanks.

"I'm gonna go outside and smoke... you want to join me, son?"

The boy followed as if on an invisible leash. The wind was picking up and it was a typical cold day in Pennsylvania.

As was my habit, I put on my tight black Leather gloves. I was surprised when he pulled out a similar pair from the inside of his jacket.

"Nothing like Leather to keep you warm, huh?" I stated.

"No, Sir."

"You never did tell me your name, son?"

"It's Chris, Sir."

"Let me punch your cigar for you, son." With that I reached over and extracted the cigar from his pocket. I noticed a rubber bulb skillfully placed around the boy's neck and hidden by the fold of his jacket.

The boy was quick to pull his jacket closed, but I knew where the rubber bulb and tubing to which it was attached led and what purpose it served.

I continued to make small talk as we puffed on our respective cigars and as the traffic whizzed past.

The boy seemed to relax a little as I continued to talk.

In short order, the washing machine's cycles were done and we returned inside, leaving our half-smoked cigars outside.

I put my clothes in a duffle bag. After all, the dryer at home still worked, or at least, I hope it did.

"If you want to finish that cigar with a shot of whiskey, son, why don't you come on over to my place?" With that, I reached inside his jacket and gave the rubber ball a couple of healthy squeezes. The boy moaned as the inflatable dildo made its presence known.

"Yes, Sir." He unloaded his clothes into a clothes basket and followed me out the door. We picked up our abandoned cigars.

Within fifteen minutes, I pulled my cycle into the yard and his Honda Civic parked next to it.

As the boy entered the back door, he had dutifully carried his wet laundry in.

"We're going to do more than laundry, son," I thought, as I offered to take the basket downstairs to the basement. I left it sitting in the laundry area and returned to the boy.

He stood where I left him in the hallway.

"Come on in, son. The whiskey is in the den."

As I poured him a healthy shot and picked up an ashtray and lighter, I had a chance to look at his boyish frame. Cute ass, slender torso. All packaged very nicely in those black jeans, rubber tee shirt, and Leather jacket.

I offered him the whiskey and we made ourselves comfortable on the Leather sofa. I stretched my arm around him, but didn't make any more immediate moves on the boy.

I put on the Terminator CD to settle his nerves – after all, looking at Arnold's naked ass and then Arnold in Leather was, I thought, stimulating foreplay for a Leatherman and his boy.

The boy seemed to concentrate on the images as he sipped the shot of whiskey and puffed on his cigar.

My cock was pulsing inside my jeans and pressing against my chaps.

My hand reached into the fold of the boy's jacket and pumped the rubber bulb. The boy's head arched backward as the surrogate dick inched up his rectum.

I withdrew my hand and pulled the boy's head toward me. I thrust my tongue in his mouth. With the other hand, I pulled his left leg over mine.

I unzipped his jeans and reached a gloved hand into his pants. A throbbing cock saluted me.

"Let's go upstairs, son." Chris followed me obediently and soon, we were rolling around in bed. My Leather and his Leather colliding.

As my dick got harder and harder, I commanded the boy to withdraw it from my pants. He needed no further instruction as he went down on it and sucked my throbbing manrod until it exploded in his mouth. He slurped up the spilled cum as if it was the finest whiskey.

After he performed that duty, I instructed him to lay on top of me and he soon shot a load on my chaps. He gratefully licked that up too.

After we had cuddled and fondled for a while, my S&M tendencies made their presence known.

"We'll now go to the basement, son. It's time for a flogging session."

The boy did not question my determination of this session, but stood up and waited for his newly-found Leatherdaddy to lead him to the workover room.

I pulled a smoke hood out of the bureau drawer and he stood obediently as I laced it tightly around his head. Tight wrist-restraints were placed on each of his wrists. I gathered my flogger and several whips and paddles from the closet of my bedroom. I lead him carefully down the basement steps, where his abandoned laundry basket sat on the dryer.

I stood in front of him and pressed my body against his. I slowly removed his Leather jacket and rubber shirt.

He stood obediently as I manacled him to the St. Andrew's cross.

I punched and lighted another cigar for each of us, inserting his into the mouth-hole of the smoke hood.

He obediently puffed as I lashed his now-naked back with the first of many rotations of floggings.

I pulled down his jeans around his knees to administer the butt paddling. The dildo was still in place and I pumped the bulb until he was twisting and turning.

"Don't worry, son, it will be replaced soon enough."

The boy was a true submissive and flinched as the lashings connected with his naked skin, but he never cried out. He stood obediently.

In between rotations, I rubbed his reddening back and ass. After fifty lashings, I attached a pair of alligators to his virgin tits. He cried out for the first time as he apparently did not have much experience with clamps. I attached them to a hook where they remained in place for the next fifty floggings. As his body flinched,

45

the clamps pulled harder and harder on his nips. I pumped up the dildo again.

Still, he stood obediently. Next, he received fifty paddlings on his tender asscheeks. After the paddling, he shook his head in gratitude as I rubbed his asscheeks with my Leather gloves.

No doubt about it, he was a good boy. The session continued until his back was crisscrossed with marks. His ass glowed a bright red as if my boy were blushing.

I checked periodically, asking him if he was still okay. He shook his head "Yes". I took the cigar out of his mouth twice as the ash lengthened.

When it looked as if it was about to fall, I demanded that he open his mouth wide and I flicked the ashes onto his tongue. Even though there was a momentary sting, the boy ate the ash and licked his lips as if he was tasting my mancum again.

"Good boy," I reassured him with each successful part of the test. He nodded his head gratefully.

I gave this boy over two hundred lashes of the flogger and over one hundred paddlings on his ass. He had proved himself as a worthy boy as I released the wrist restraints. I held him against my Leathered body as he repeatedly thanked me for the session. I rubbed my gloved hands against his reddened back and ass. Through the smoke hood, his lips nuzzled my neck and cheek.

Not so gently, I removed the dildo from his ass and inserted a gloved fist up his ass.

I continued to molest his ass and pull on his aching tits. It only seemed to make the boy more anxious to please me, rubbing his hands over my Leathers, kissing me and rubbing his hooded head against my chest. I was horny as hell for the next session, but rationalized that there was to be no more lashings for this session. He was a good boy.

We went back upstairs and continued to watch the Terminator. His head rested against my shoulder as he relaxed.

After an interlude of relaxation, the grateful boy slipped down to the floor and began massaging my cock which was fully extended in my jeans.

"May I, Daddy?"

I rubbed his head, encased in the Leather hood, and shook my head "Yes". As I continued to puff on my cigar, the boy tongued my extended dick in the jeans.

I undid my pants and pulled my throbbing cock out of its denim enclosure.

The grateful boy took my cock in his mouth and 'smoked' it as if it was a fine cigar.

"Good boy," as I exploded in his mouth for the second time.

The next morning, the boy left with his wet laundry in the untouched basket. Before he left, I sorted through it and discarded all the pairs of tidy whities. As my boy, he would never need them again. I went to work that morning in damp jeans and a tee – they were damp, but they were clean.

Two weeks later, I had exhausted my supply of tees and wearable jeans. The replacement belts for the washing machine still had not come. I loaded my laundry into my saddlebags and headed for the public laundromat and "Oh, damn, did I forget my wallet again?"

I knew for a fact that Chris would be there – with two loaded baskets. I was more interested in one than the other.

I will never think of public laundromats as anything but fine establishments from now on.

RIDE 'EM, DREAM COWBOY!

Seth was dreaming. Seth was dreaming for the nine millionth time. Seth had more erotic dreams than anyone else on the planet. Seth had coupled with lawyers, doctors, garbage men, firemen – in short, anyone with a dick between their legs. The smile on Seth's face indicated that this was a successful partnership with the 'man of his dreams' and he slept on.

Seth usually didn't remember too many details of his dreams the next morning. But when the telephone woke him abruptly at 6:45 am, he snatched the fragments of his last dream, stored them in his memory bank, and answered the phone. It was his friend, Scott, from Chicago, who always wanted morning sex over the phone. Seth obliged and both men worked their cocks into a hardened frenzy, while they made crude suggestions to each other about what they would do if they were in the same bed. They had never met. They had made contact through a sex line and enjoyed one another's J/O calls.

After satisfying Scott and licking the jism off his dick and belly with his finger, Seth got out of bed. While he brushed his teeth, the fragments of his dream came back to him. The dream was somehow different than all the others. He was standing by a split rail fence. That much he knew. He couldn't see himself in the recalled dream, but he was sure it was himself. There were miles and miles of nothingness except an occasional rock or cactus. The sky was a brilliant blue, almost hurtful to the eye. As he looked off into the distance, he saw a rider on a horse. Just a pin-dot on the horizon, but he could tell it was a cowboy.

The next fragment came to him while he was fixing his morning coffee. Shit, he was so groggy he could hardly move before having his coffee. He saw the horse turn abruptly. It was then that he got a real look at the rider. The cowboy wore Western boots in a fancy red and white design, Leather chaps of golden tan with a deep fringe down the length of the leg, faded blue jeans, a red bandana around his neck, and, of course, his ten-gallon hat. Seth knew there was something missing, but he couldn't quite remember. He sipped his coffee and mused about the dream while watching the sun slowly rise in the sky.

Traffic was beginning to pick up in front of his apartment and he rallied himself to get ready. Seth worked in an office and started to work at nine. The commute was at least forty-five minutes.

Shit, he thought, *I'm gonna be late, as usual.* He put on the usual white shirt, navy blue pants, and a bland tie, so he would look like all the other clones in the office. *Ah, what they don't know won't hurt them...* he thought as he zipped his pants open and put a metal cockring around the base of his nuts and cock. He really enjoyed having a cockring in place.

While on the interstate, Seth tried to remember more details of his dream. It really had him intrigued. It seemed right at the front of his mind. He fondled his cock and said, "I sure as hell hope I dream the same dream tonight."

He did. He dreamed the same dream for the next four nights, never quite being able to remember what it was or why it was so different.

On the fifth night, Seth went out for a few beers with friends. His friend, Rob, wanted to spend the night, but Seth begged off. Seth was extremely relaxed and horny and wishing that he had asked Rob to stay when he crawled into bed. He fell asleep almost instantly and dreamed the usual erotic stuff: fucking a doctor on the examination table, a lawyer on the judge's bench while the judge watched, etc...

Then the cowboy came. He rode out of the sunset. The dream was just like a three-dimensional movie. The cowboy seemed to ride right out of the screen and Seth could hear the horse's hooves pounding on the bedroom floor. The cowboy carried a bullwhip, a detail that Seth had missed until now. He was dressed in the golden tan Leather chaps, the cowboy hat, the bandana, the red and white cowboy boots, and the faded jeans.

Seth seemed to lean forward in his sleep to savor every detail. Well, for one, the cowboy had no shirt on, showing off a big, beautiful muscular chest with lots of hair and big, chewy nipples. Seth licked his lips in his sleep. The cowboy circled the fenced enclosure they both now seemed to be in. As he turned his back on Seth, Seth noticed one other detail. The blue jeans were ripped and the man's beautiful asscheeks were hanging out.

Ride 'em, cowboy!

At this point, Seth woke up. *Shit,* he thought, *only ten more minutes and I would have creamed over this dream, Shit.*

For the next several nights, Seth dreamed the same segment of the cowboy dream. The cowboy and horse would swing around in a fenced enclosure and Seth would get a close-up of the cowboy's ass. This was all fine and good, but, hell, he wanted more!

Finally, almost two weeks after Seth had had the first dream, he mellowed out with a big black cigar, a couple of strong drinks, and poppers. "If this doesn't do it, nothing will," he mused. Seth drifted off to sleep and almost immediately had the usual dreams – this time with his algebra teacher from high school and an Army private with Grade A, Extra Large privates. Seth licked his lips and stroked his cock absently in his sleep.

"Yahoo! Ride 'em, cowboy!"

The Army private's head jerked upward, letting Seth's dick slide out of his mouth. "What the hell was that, man?" the private asked. At this point, Seth only wanted the private to continue his sucking action, but by the time his sleeping mind returned to the private, the man had evaporated into the netherworld.

Seth was once again within the fenced enclosure and his dream cowboy was riding toward him at a fast and furious pace. The cowboy came closer and closer, revealing the same beautiful tan suede chaps and red and white boots. Seth could now clearly see the bullwhip in the cowboy's hand. The horse reared abruptly and performed a ninety-degree turn, kicking up a cloud of dust that stung Seth's eyes.

"Yahoo! A little doggie to rope!"

At this point, the cowboy threw the end of the bullwhip high over his head and snapped it forward. CRACK! sounded the whip and Seth's cock and balls were wrapped securely within the tail of the bullwhip. His manrod was hard and his balls burned with the sensation of the rough Leather encircling them. Seth moaned in his sleep and begged the man upstairs to let the fantasy continue.

The next thing he knew, Seth was being dragged around the corral on his naked ass by the bullwhip around his cock and balls. "Shit, this hurts...," he muttered. Seconds later, a loud ringing sounded the end of the dream and the beginning of another day.

Seth had a hard time getting out of bed. His nuts felt like they were coated in layers of Ben-Gay and it was hard to move without touching them to his inner thighs. "Ooh, shit!" he groaned as he eased out of bed and hobbled to the shower. As he showered he examined the whip burns that appeared quite clearly around the base of his nuts and down the length of his cock. His ass clearly had burn marks all over it, he saw them in the mirror.

"How the hell...?"

That day at work, Seth did not wear a cockring, but instead wore two pairs of cotton undershorts. They didn't ease the burning much, but it helped... a little. He couldn't stop thinking about this latest dream that had somehow become a reality.

Rob stopped by Seth's cubicle, "Hey, Buddy, you seem awfully distracted today – you didn't even see that new hunk up on the fourth floor. Jesus, would I like to tie him up!"

Seth, who was trying to find a position in his chair where his nuts and ass didn't burn like hellfire itself, hadn't even heard Rob, but answered absently, "Yeah, I know what you mean..." The rest of the day passed without Seth accomplishing much. The burning eased off by the end of the day and as he returned home he fervently hoped that the cowboy would return that night.

That evening, he put on his Leather pants and crawled into bed. He hoped that if he were going to be dragged around a corral, at least he would protect his ass. Once again, Seth drifted off into the netherworld of dreams and quickly sucked off two boys he knew in college, both of whom were football heroes. They were wearing their shoulder pads and their sweaty, smelly jockstraps. Seth was on the offensive and the two boys always seemed to tackle him, one grabbing his nuts and the other twisting his tits. The shoulder pads were jammed into his face and underneath his ass. It was a good fantasy, but it didn't even get him hard this night.

As Seth assumed the position of quarterback and threw a spiral down the field to some unseen receiver, the two brutes ran toward him. Just as they were ready to tackle Seth the quarterback, their heads snapped backward as they collectively heard, "Yahoo, Hoss, I'm gonna rope me a doggie tonight!"

The football players and the field melted away, replaced by the same corral. Seth was once again within the enclosure and his dream cowboy and horse came galloping out of the sunset. As the horse approached, Seth could see that the bullwhip was in place on the saddle horn and a lariat was being twirled by the cowboy high over his head.

Seth tried to run away from the cowboy, but to no avail. The lariat swung neatly over his head and arms and landed securely on his pecs. It jerked him abruptly to the ground, his feet flying out from under him. Dirt and dust greeted Seth as he landed squarely in the middle of the corral. The cowboy was off his horse in a flash, tightening the hold of the lariat around Seth's chest.

"Yahoo! I caught me one!" the cowboy hollered. Seth struggled to free himself, but the lariat had a very firm grip around his chest. "Now ya just stop that, boy, you're my prize and I'm gonna tie you up."

With that, the cowboy pulled another length of rope off his saddle and securely tied Seth's hands behind his back. He then turned Seth over on his back as easily as if he were flicking a fly off his horse. Seth's back was arched. The cowboy pulled the bullwhip off his saddle horn and strode ten paces away.

"Now, boy, let's have a little fun," the cowboy drawled, "I ain't had a doggie in a long time." He snapped the bullwhip and once again Seth felt the burning sensation of raw Leather around his cock and balls. The pain was intense, but, despite the pain, Seth's cock was throbbing.

"Aah, boy, I see we got ya excited, don't we?" the cowboy taunted.

Seth was unable to speak, but watched as the cowboy pulled out a big plug of tobacco, inserting it in his left cheek. He chewed on it for a few minutes. He stepped closer to Seth and planted one of his fancy red and white boots squarely at the base of Seth's stomach, the tip of the boot touching Seth's throbbing cock. He shifted the boot, grinding the heel into Seth's stomach. The toe of the boot jerked Seth's cock back and forth. It was so erotic that Seth knew he would cream at any moment.

"I know what you're thinking, boy, but I ain't gonna let ya jack off yet," the cowboy said, "Ya'll forget, I'm your dream, huh? But *I'm* controlling it and it's when I say ya jack that ya jack off." He removed his boot from Seth's anatomy.

He walked away, trailing the bullwhip's length after him. The bullwhip began pulling on the cock and balls. Seth groaned as the pressure increased. His cock was being pulled steadily upward. The cowboy dangled the handle of the bullwhip back and forth, alternately jerking Seth's dick up and down.

The cowboy whistled for his horse, which stood nearby, grazing on small clumps of grass within the enclosure. The horse responded obediently. The cowboy tied the end of the bullwhip to the saddle horn.

"All right, Hoss, we're gonna see if your ass is made of Leather or not," he grinned. Inexplicably, Seth realized that he had lost his Leather pants and was buck naked in the dream.

The cowboy remounted his horse and jabbed his spurs into the horse's flanks. The horse reared up and then galloped away, dragging Seth behind like a sack of flour.

Seth yelled, "SHIT!" as loud as he could, but the wind rushing past him swallowed it as quickly as it was out of his mouth.

The cowboy looked back at him and yelled, "Ya'll can yell as loud as ya want, Hoss. Nobody can hear ya. Take it like a cowboy!"

The horse circled the corral endless times and, by the fourth or fifth time, Seth couldn't even feel his ass. He was sure it was bloodied and raw, however. Not to mention his cock and balls, which would probably detach at any moment.

Wake up, stupid! Seth pleaded with his own subconscious. *Ring alarm! This hurts like hell!*

"All right, Hoss, we gonna show ya a little trick now. Hold on!" With that, the cowboy spurred his horse forward, galloping toward the far end of the enclosure.

Holy Shit! Seth thought. *We're gonna jump that damned fence. Goodbye, manhood! Hello, castration...*

The horse, rider, and 'passenger' cleared the fence and rode toward the sunset. By this time, Seth had given up hope of ever waking up or surviving intact. They rode for what seemed hours, jumping over jagged rocks and prickly cacti, all of which left their indelible marks on Seth's tortured body.

Finally, as abruptly as they had started, they stopped. The cowboy reined the horse in and tied it to a small sapling. The sapling overhung a crystalline pond. Seth gazed at it, thinking it a cruel illusion. The cowboy dismounted and came over to his unwilling passenger. He shot a gob of tobacco into Seth's face.

"What do you think, Hoss, am I the man of your dreams?"

Seth, not knowing what to expect, replied, "Yes, Sir." This time his voice was audible. He said no more, but lowered his head and waited for the next punishment.

"Shit, ya'll did pretty well there, Hoss."

With that the cowboy came over and stood over Seth. Seth once again noticed the cowboy's clothing. The red and white cowboy boots, the fringed tan suede chaps, and the faded blue jeans, which were ripped. And, of course, there was that cowboy's handsome chest. Despite all he had been through, Seth's cock was saluting his cowboy.

The cowboy turned around and squatted over Seth's face. "Go to it, boy," he ordered, "Explore my ass with your tongue." He ripped the butt of the jeans open even further than they had been.

Seth strained forward and reached his tongue into the cowboy's glory hole. His tongue seemed to reach into the inner depths of the man's beautiful butt. Seth began to enjoy the task demanded of him and began stroking the ass and asscheeks with his tongue. He could now view the chaps that fit the cowboy like a second skin. They outlined the asscheeks and caressed the muscular thighs of the cowboy. The fringes tickled Seth's naked tits and belly. His nipples became firm and hard. The cowboy continued to gyrate and had unbuttoned his jeans so he could stroke his meat while being serviced in the rear.

After a good, long time, the cowboy turned around. His manrod was fully extended and throbbing up and down. As he turned around, the cowboy jerked on the bullwhip, causing a great sensation of pain to Seth's cock and balls.

"Just don't forget who's in charge, Hoss!" the cowboy growled.

The cowboy dangled his meat over Seth's chest. He rubbed the head of his cock against Seth's nipples. Seth shuddered with the intensity of the feeling and knew that he would have to jerk soon. The cowboy continued to rub his cock against Seth's nipples until Seth thought he would go wild or worse, wake up.

I didn't mean it, man, he prayed, *I don't want to wake up, not now!*

The cowboy inched forward, inserting his impressive manrod into Seth's mouth. Seth gagged at first because the man was so huge. Slowly, though, he let his throat relax and was able to accommodate the cowboy's dick in his throat. He sucked on it and sucked on it, all the while staring into the beautiful blue eyes of the cowboy.

After ten minutes or so, the cowboy yelled, "Yahoo! Hoss! I'm gonna shoot...ah, man, my jism is gonna flow..."

Seth sucked harder on the man's dick and, once again, the cowboy's hips gyrated back and forth, just as if he were on a mechanical bull. His hands gripped the sides of Seth's head firmly.

"HOSS! You're pretty damned fine!" The cowboy started to work his dick up and down Seth's throat as Seth continued to suck harder and harder. "Yahoo!" the man yelled again, "Yahoo!" And with that, the cowboy shot a wad down Seth's throat. They both sighed, breathing heavily.

Seth closed his eyes. This had to pure heaven as far as he was concerned and he hoped that he never woke up. He could do this all the time.

The cowboy stood up and jerked on the bullwhip, once again jerking Seth's cock and balls until they burned with pain. This time, however, they also burned with pleasure. The cowboy continued to manipulate the bullwhip back and forth, each time creating a new threshold of pain over which Seth now willingly stepped.

"Yeah, cowboy, jerk 'em right off my fuckin' body," Seth moaned with pleasure, "Yeah, make 'em burn."

The cowboy got down on his knees and shot a wad of tobacco juice all over Seth's privates. The liquid burned on the tortured cock and balls, but again pleasure and pain were intimately intertwined. "Oh, yeah, man, it feels so good," Seth moaned.

The cowboy began manipulating Seth's cock in his roughened hands. He slapped the dick against one of his hands. Then he would roll it in his hands like a piece of modeling clay. He spit some more tobacco juice on the cock and balls until they glistened shiny and brown in the desert sun.

"Now, before I suck ya off, Hoss," drawled the cowboy, "I wanna see what ya got on the other side of this body of yours."

With that, he flipped Seth over like he was a flapjack.

The man spit on his two hands with the same tobacco juice and then stuck one, two, and then three fingers up Seth's ass. "Hey, Hoss, ya know your ass is pretty dirty. It looks like ya been dragged all over town," he snorted, laughing at his own joke. "I don't know that I want to get my fingers dirty, but I got just the solution."

He reached for the handle of the bullwhip and, without any sort of lubrication or warning, jammed it up Seth's ass. Seth let out a yelp as the wooden handle reached up his asshole. At this point, Seth was so involved with the fantasy, he was sure it was the cowboy's dick itself. The cowboy waggled the handle backward and forward, in and out, and pretty soon, Seth's ass had relaxed and accepted the whole handle of the bullwhip.

Leaving the handle in Seth's ass, the cowboy once again tumbled Seth over. Seth's dick was hard and throbbing. This time, the man lay down on top of Seth in a sixty-nine position. His cock teased Seth's lips. The man's sunbaked chest slid up and down Seth's chest and thighs. His mouth encircled Seth's cock.

"Yahoo!" he yelled, "You're a cowboy now, Hoss! Ride 'em, cowboy!" With that, he yanked on the bullwhip, tightening the grip on Seth's balls and dick, and then swallowed the dick, balls and their Leather enclosure.

Holy Shit, thought Seth, *This feels so damned good... last forever, please!*

The cowboy's tongue trailed every inch of Leather, moistening it with tobacco and juice and saliva. He tongued every inch of exposed genitalia. His lips closed down on the head of Seth's cock. He started sucking with such force that Seth was certain that if his set didn't drop off because of the bullwhip, they would be pulled off by the vacuuming motion of the cowboy's tongue. His cock throbbed harder and harder as the cowboy continued to suck.

Easing off for a moment, the cowboy yelled, "Here it comes, cowboy! Ride that hoss!" He swallowed Seth's cock, tonguing the balls and the Leather surrounding them.

The cowboy's dick was once again engorged and Seth was going up and down on it as fast and furious as he could. *This is what dreams are made of,* he thought, *but it's the real thing!*

"Yahoo!" yelled the cowboy as he dug his spurs into Seth's naked shoulders. With that, he sucked on Seth's cock and Seth exploded a manload of jism down the cowboy's throat. The cowboy simultaneously shot a load down Seth's eager throat. The next ten minutes were silent except for the hungry lapping of men, anxious to get the last drops of cum.

BRRRNNNGGG!!!!

Seth snapped to attention. He was once again in his own bed. He struggled out of bed, his entire body on fire. The Leather pants he had fallen asleep in were in a heap on the floor. As he crossed to the bathroom to take a piss, he looked in the mirror. His cock and balls once again had burn marks. His ass was a bloodied mess. Rope burns on his wrists. Dried jism was evident on his chin. His body was streaked with dirt.

As his eyes adjusted to the new day, he thought, *What the hell?* He leaned forward to view his face more closely in the mirror. *Now how am I going to explain this at the office?* There was the distinct mark of a branding iron on his left cheek. The mark read "GP".

Ride 'em, cowboy.

This article originally appeared in **CUIR: For LeatherMen By LeatherMen, Issue 2 (1992)** under my pseudonym Thad Rinehart.

CANED AND ABLE

"Patrick Joseph Gallagher – you have disrupted this class once again. Matthew O'Boyle, escort Patrick to Father O'Hara's office with this note". Sister Margaret Rose hastily wrote a note and handed it to Matthew. The two young men trooped up the hallway.

Patrick was always in trouble at school and was no stranger to Father O'Hara's office. His college career was in shambles, he had been kicked out of two colleges and St. Peter's College was a last ditch effort by his parents to secure an education for their troubled son.

Matthew remained silent, but Patrick emitted a series of curse words that made the younger Matthew blush.

The boys arrived at the door of the Father and Matthew hastily left after knocking solemnly on the Father's door for admittance.

Father O'Hara opened the door and was not surprised to see Patrick.

"Oh, Patrick, come in, son."

The Father sat in his chair behind the meticulously-arranged desk and indicated that Patrick should sit in the chair in front of the desk. Father O'Hara was a man of seventy-five years and tried to serve as a grandfather to many of the boys in St. Peter's in Boston. The gentle tone in his voice admonished Patrick for his disregard of the rules at St. Peter's after reading Sister's note. Patrick listened stoically as the Father admonished him.

He was to be sequestered in his room for the next two weeks and to write an essay on the life of Saul and his conversion on the road to Damascus. Father hoped that it would provide some inspiration for the troubled boy who had been punished on so many occasions. He had his doubts, however. He prayed with the boy about it and hoped that this would provide the necessary motivation for a change of heart.

As it turned out, it was Father O'Hara's last week at the college. He died quietly in his sleep. In the confusion of the transition, Patrick's sentence was forgotten and he was told to return to class. The Parish Church which administered the college quickly replaced O'Hara with Father Dominick, an imposing six foot tall priest with black hair and ice blue eyes. Father Dominick was briefed by the instructors at the school and Patrick's name came up more than once.

Barely a week had gone by before Patrick was sent to the Father's office.

The Father sat behind his desk and did not offer Patrick a seat.

"Patrick, son, it seems you are a discipline problem within the school and we need to amend that as quickly as possible." The Father stood up and held in his hand a length of cane.

"Patrick, son, lower your pants and your underpants."

"What, Father?"

"I don't mumble, son, do it, NOW!"

The boy, never having encountered such forcefulness in the school, quickly pulled down his pants, and soon, his buttocks were crisscrossed with the marks of the fifteen canings he had received as a result of his transgression.

The boy returned to class. The memory of the caning was fresh in his mind and he replayed the unblinking gaze of the Father's eyes over and over in his mind. His ass burned from the canings and he was the model student for the next several days.

At night, as he rubbed his sore ass, Patrick replayed the scene in his mind repeatedly.

A week went by, and Patrick kept his nose clean. After morning devotions on the eighth day, however, the boys were seated in Sister Margaret Rose's class. Someone from the back of the room threw a book which, as Sister turned around from the chalkboard, hit her squarely in the nose and caused it to bleed.

"All right, who did that?"

The boys remained silent.

"Patrick, was it you?"

"No, Sister..."

"Don't lie to me, boy..."

"No, Sister, I really didn't..."

"We'll see what Father has to say about this." Before Patrick could protest his innocence, Sister had written a note and Patrick was escorted by Thomas Fitzgerald to Father Dominick's office.

"Well, Son, I see that our initial meeting had little effect on you..."

"Father Dominick, I did not do this..."

"Well, we'll see if a little additional punishment will yield the confession we need... you know the routine, Son, down with your pants..."

With that, Father Dominick caned Patrick with twenty lashes. The young man cried out and turned several times to plead for the Father to stop, but his gaze was met with unblinking eyes. The eyes seemed to twinkle as each lash was administered.

Despite a toughness developed over his first twenty years on earth, Patrick cried and rubbed his sore buttocks when it was finished.

"Now, Son, you know what you will receive each time you transgress.." Father did concede a bit, and rubbed the boy's sore ass with his big hands. They caressed the tender flesh as he pulled up the young man's pants. Patrick's cock hardened at the touch of the priest's hands. Patrick was returned to class and doubled up his jacket to sit on for the remainder of the classes.

That night, Patrick dreamed. He dreamed that he was doing the caning on Father Dominick's ass. He woke with a hard-on and despite the warnings from the Catholic instructors, he masturbated. He felt an erotic awakening from the canings and being at the mercy of the substantial Father Dominick.

Over the next several months, Patrick purposely got into trouble.

Father Dominick obligingly caned the unrepentant boy. The boy watched Father Dominick's face and there was often a smile on his face as he administered the canings. On several occasions, the Father's hand disappeared into the black robe he wore. Patrick noticed a substantial tenting of the robe where the Father's dick was. "Father was getting off on beating my ass," reasoned Patrick. Patrick, of course, never challenged the Father's authority. He never talked to anyone about his theories concerning Father.

At night, however, he masturbated more frequently, thinking of Father Dominick.

One Saturday morning, Father was in the confessional hearing the varied sins of the parishioners of the church.

Patrick saw his opportunity and crawled on hands and knees into the booth. He carefully lifted the long, black robe of Father Dominick and was greeted with an immense penis dangling between the Father's legs. The boy couldn't help but notice that the priest was wearing black Leather boots buckled at the knee.

Patrick tenderly licked the piss slit of the Father's cockhead. The Father's legs clamped together as the boy's tongue touched the cockhead, but slowly relaxed. The Father was in the middle of a woman's lengthy confession and could not easily interrupt her.

Father's hand, which was covered in a skin-tight black Leather glove, came down and felt the head of the boy underneath his robe. He slowly pushed the boy's head toward his crotch until the boy's mouth was more fully engaged on the shaft of the dick.

The boy sucked the manmeat and then sought out the man's loose balls. The man's head arched back as the boy's tonguing made Father fully erect.

"What a magnificent mancock!" the boy thought as he continued to please the Father. The confession done, Father closed the confessional screen. He then unbuttoned his robe, to reveal a massive chest with rose-colored nipples. His mantits were outlined with a Leather harness The boy couldn't resist and sucked and licked the titflesh too.

Father pulled the boy toward him and the man and boy kissed long and hard with their tongues reaching deep into each other's throats.

Father leaned forward and whispered, "You are going to go with me and meet some of my friends."

Patrick had little choice but to answer "Yes, Father."

At the end of the session when Father Dominick's cum coursed down the boy's throat, the boy was told to pack a few items for a weekend.

Father encountered Sister Margaret Rose in the hallway, "I'm taking Patrick with me to a retreat for the weekend... he and I need to discuss his sinful being."

Sister Margaret Rose replied, "I hope for his sake it will change him forever, Father."

"It will, trust me on this, Sister," Father said with a twinkle in his eye.

The man and boy departed, driving approximately two hours. Father's right hand was casually laid around the boy's shoulder. It would occasionally migrate south, squeezing the boy's nipple or crotch. Patrick relished it – Father Dominick had provided lots of wet dreams and now he and the Father were together.

They arrived at a small house out in the country. The boy was ordered to strip and to lay on a platform covered in Leather sheeting. Fairly soon, Father Dominick appeared, but not in his usual black robe. He now wore a Leather hood, Leather gloves, and his tall, black Leather boots. Patrick recognized the icy blue stare of the priest's eyes behind the hood and he also recognized the man's considerable penis which hung between the priest's legs.

Soon, other men filtered in, wearing similar attire.

"Boy Patrick, these are Father Peter and Father Dick and our associates. They call me Father Dominator. We are the Order of Leather Priests who like to fuck college boys like you." The men laughed.

With that, each man reached over and slapped Patrick with their length of cane held in their Leather gloved hands. "You have sinned, boy," they each said as they delivered their canings.

"Yes, Fathers, I know I have sinned, please reprimand me some more..." Patrick whispered. His dick was hardening as the delicious beatings continued, "More, Fathers, more!" he moaned. The men obliged and the canings continued into the night. The men pulled out a series of paddles and floggers and worked the boy over until his body had a crisscrossing of red marks. The boy was then escorted off the table, kneeling before each priest and servicing their cocks.

The Father and boy continued to play throughout Patrick's school career, with a number of weekends at the retreat for similar sessions with the Order. Some of the students thought it odd that Patrick would now go to the Father's office on his own, and the canings could be heard far down the hallway. Patrick had changed his scholastic attitude, however, and graduated near the top of his class. It was on graduation day that he announced his intentions to enter the Priesthood.

Ten years have elapsed since Patrick attended St. Peter's College. He is now a priest for a small Catholic college in Philadelphia.

He and Father Dominick have remained in close contact.

A knock was heard on the door of Father Patrick's study.

"In," he ordered.

"Father Patrick, I have sinned."

"Have you now, son? You, of course, know the routine." He pulled black Leather gloves from his desk drawer.

Father Dominick pulled off his robe and the caning from Father Patrick began..

A Boner Book

CONVERSION

Upon opening his email that afternoon, the Leatherdaddy should have known better.

There was a message from his Leatherbuddy Dan. It simply stated that Dan's cousin was spending the weekend in the Leatherdaddy's town. Dan asked his Leatherbuddy to look after his cousin. The Leatherman assumed that that meant he show the boy his version of pleasure – Leather S&M sex. And the Daddy had been down that dismal road before with inexperienced boys – with the usual pathetic results. However, Dan was a good Leatherbuddy and the two had enjoyed many sessions together. The Leatherman quickly returned Dan's message for details. Dan replied, "a strapping boy, recently came out as gay, haven't seen him in years. Told me he was up for new experiences. Eager to learn. Here's his email..."

The Daddy shot off a message to the potential boy, giving him directions to his secluded place of male debauchery and began to anticipate a protracted session.

By six, the boy had returned his message, indicating he was in town and would arrive shortly.

The Daddy's toolshed was in readiness (as usual) and he had already exchanged his business suit for his real suit of business – his Leather uniform. He sat on his back porch, with his booted feet hiked up on the porch railing. He absently played with his loaded codpiece while he dragged on a Montecristo cigar.

A car pulled into the driveway at 6:45. It was true that the boy had obeyed the directive in wearing a white tee shirt and jeans, but he was wearing a cashmere sweater knotted around his neck and expensive running shoes. As he approached the porch, a strong scent of cologne offended the Leatherdaddy's olfactory senses. A number of gold chains were wrapped around the boy's neck and wrist. It was true – he was strapping, over six feet and nice pecs, but "Holy Christ, I'm gonna make this boy into a Leatherboy?" the Leatherman thought, questioning his own abilities at working miracles.

The boy climbed the porch steps.

"Hi, I'm Doug, Dan's cousin..."

"Yeah, I guessed who you were, boy..."

The boy reeked of cologne as he neared the Leatherman and the man held him off at arm's length.

"Oooh, Leather, I have a pair of Leather jeans that I just bought to wear to the bar..."

"I'll just bet you did, boy."

The boy looked slightly perplexed as the Daddy motioned for him to drop to his knees. When the boy resisted, he was forcibly pushed down to the porch flooring.

"Dan said you would show me what life was like in the country. Did I do something wrong?," the boy questioned.

"A whole hell of a lot of things wrong, boy."

With some forced convincing, the man directed the boy to the back lawn. The cashmere sweater was discarded on the ground, as the boy gasped. He lunged for it, "I paid over two hundred dollars for that..."

The Daddy made a point of stepping on the sweater with his military boots, thus, leaving a muddy footprint on the back of the sweater. The sleeve of the sweater ripped as the boy tried to retrieve the sweater.

"You won't need it for awhile, son. Leave it where it is..."

The boy looked doubtful, but the man grabbed the boy by the back of the neck and got right in his face, "You will do as ordered, son, now, leave the fucking sweater where it is." The sweater remained as a crumpled pile on the lawn.

"Take your fucking shoes off, boy." The man stood over the boy until the boy had obeyed his directive. "Christ, the boy has argyle socks on...," the man thought. "Socks too, boy."

The boy obeyed. The boy was ordered to lay on the grass and the Leatherman stood over the prone boy. He nearly choked from the smell of the cologne.

With that, the Leatherman pulled out his cock and pissed all over the boy. The boy sputtered as his clothing was soaked with the smell of strong man piss.

"What are you doing?" the boy whimpered.

"Making you into a Leatherboy, now shut up, you dickhead..."

The boy glared at the man, but did not immediately respond. His face registered surprise and disgust all at the same time. "I'll have to do laundry as soon as I get home," the boy thought.

The Leatherman's stream of piss lasted for a good long time. After all, he had relaxed with a couple of beers before the boy had arrived.

The boy's tee shirt was soaked with piss, revealing a nice set of nips and a very handsome chest.

"You work out, son?"

"Yes, I do," the boy responded hesitantly, "three times a week... And I run five miles a day."

"Then, why are you such a damned faggot?" the Leatherman questioned, thinking, "This is Dan's cousin? Wait until I get his ass..."

The boy began to respond, but was caught off guard when the weight of a shiny military boot was planted firmly in the middle of his chest.

"Lick my boot, boy."

"Whaaat?" the boy questioned, "I've never licked a boot before..."

"You're gonna start now, son..." The Leatherman's weight shifted to the boot in the middle of the boy's chest.

"I said NOW!, boy."

The boy made a half-hearted attempt, with a look of disgust on his face.

The Leatherman bent over and said, "And look as if you enjoy it, boy." He blew a stream of smoke from the cigar into the boy's face. The boy began coughing.

The Leatherman just laughed. The boy, realizing he better comply, began the task.

For a first – timer, the boy did a pretty decent job. He finally looked up for the man's approval.

"Not a bad job, son," the Leatherman remarked, and was met with a slight smile from the boy.

"Now for the other boot."

The boy groaned but began licking the other boot with a stronger sense of purpose. When that was accomplished, the Leatherman inspected his boots.

"Good boy. Stand up."

The boy obeyed and the Daddy drew the boy to him. He kissed the boy and fondled the boy's muscular arms.

"You're a nice-looking boy. Take off your shirt." The boy complied.

"Very nice, son." The man rubbed his gloved hands over the boy's chest, arms and back.

"This is nice... this is more what I had in mind," the boy remarked between long kisses.

After a few minutes, the Leatherman drew away from the boy. "This is only a precursor to the events of the day, son... Follow me."

The boy, barefoot and shirtless, followed the man to a row of hedges. He was anticipating a hot tub where they could wash off the disgusting smell of urine.

The boy's jaw dropped as he was led inside a toolshed and viewed a workover table with restraints and chains, and a wall full of whips and paddles.

"Oh, no, this is nothing like I thought it would be like...," the boy began, before he was inelegantly hoisted on to the table. Being such a big boy, this wasn't an easy task. And he wasn't going willingly. He struggled as the Leatherman attempted to place bondage ropes around his torso. Wrist restraints were next, followed by ankle restraints. The boy continued to struggle and the chains were being wrenched until the Leatherdaddy thought the boy would pull them right out of the ceiling.

"Relax, son." as the man slapped the boy across the face, "You'll enjoy it more..."

"Let me out of here, you sadistic pervert...I'm calling the cops. HELP!"

The Daddy had no recourse but to stuff a black Leather dildo gag in the boy's mouth, strapping the gag behind the boy's neck.

The boy continued to struggle, pulling the chains violently.

The Daddy was getting angrier by the moment, eventually hauling off with a Leather paddle, spanking the boy's ass repeatedly.

That seemed to settle the boy down and he relaxed momentarily. Or perhaps he was too scared to react.

That gave the Leatherman time to tighten the bondage ropes and restraints until the boy was nicely trussed into place.

As he looked into the boy's eyes, they were venomous and registered a rage at the position he was now in.

The boy continued a muffled, mouthy tirade for quite some time.

The paddling continued, intensifying, until the boy was concentrating on the strokes of the paddle. He flinched from side to side, moaning softly, but by now, his feet were hoisted in the air, and his ass was in a more suitable position for the paddling which continued.

Despite his protest, the Leatherdaddy noticed a mound which had developed in the boy's fancy ass jeans.

"Well, son, it seems your protests aren't all legitimate, now, are they?"

The Daddy unzipped the boy's jeans and reached his gloved hand into them. He pulled out a very healthy cock and two pendulous balls.

"Very nice, son, very nice..." He began massaging the boy's equipment, and despite any reservations the boy still had, his cock grew hard and firm under the expert handling of the Leatherman.

As the man continued to massage the boy's meat, the boy did relax and a smile slowly appeared on his face.

"Yowww..." the boy's muffled cry emerged, as the Daddy began to whip the cock and balls with a Leather strap. The boy shook his head violently, but to no avail, the Leatherdaddy was having too much fun and wasn't going to pay any attention to the boy's protests.

As the session progressed, the Leatherdaddy alternated between slapping the boy's cock and paddling his ass.

The boy's cock throbbed.

"Don't you cum, boy, or there will be hell to pay," the Daddy warned. The boy's eyes were pleading at this point.

The Daddy knew that the boy would shoot a load soon and he relished the thought of the retribution for it.

Within a few minutes, the boy's cock erupted, spewing a healthy flow of jism all over the boy's chest.

He was rewarded with a slap across the face. "I told you not to cum, asshole."

The boy began whimpering, shaking his head, tears welled up in his eyes.

The Daddy turned toward the workbench and greased up his right glove.

The boy seemed unaware of what was to come and once again, let out a yowl as the Leathered fist invaded his boyhole.

The boy protested as best he could, but finally gave in to the Leatherman's exploration.

The boy, covered in piss and drying cum, lay silently as the man removed his fist and inserted his own hardened cock up the boy's fuckhole.

That was three months ago. Doug is now my Leatherboy. Three months of intense training and Doug now wears Leather as proudly as his Daddy. The cashmere sweater is used as a jack rag and the boy no longer wears cologne (I won't allow it). Instead, he embraces the smell of mancum and piss, and a body scented with all-day sessions in Leather. Dan is soon to arrive for the weekend and so, we will be headed out to the toolshed to work over his cousin. The boy is looking forward to it. And, I have a little score to settle with Dan. His ass is mine as well. In anticipation of the session, I have greased up two gloves.

GOLDEN BOY

I was sleazy and horny that afternoon.

Dressed in my jock, chaps, boots, gloves and Muir cap, I strolled on my property. It was secluded and so I was able to strut around with my ass hanging out without fear of exposure to my neighbors. My only neighbor was a small creek which I waded across to play in the woods. If I had a boy, he got tied to a tree there and flogged and molested.

This afternoon, I was alone. I was absently massaging my cock and balls through the Leather jock. Pulling on the nipclamps, wiggling the dildo shoved up my ass.

And, of course, smoking a fresh cigar.

It was a delicious feeling – I had just had a really good session with a bottom from D.C. and was regretting that he had to go back to D.C. I could have played for hours more but he had obligations at home.

I was leaning against a sturdy walnut tree, massaging my cock more vigorously when I heard a noise behind me.

I turned, only to find a handsome young man wading in the creek with his golden retriever.

He startled me, but after all I was on my own property.

"Sorry, Sir," he began, "I didn't realize anybody was out here..."

"That's okay, Buddy," as I backed against the tree, pressing my ass against it.

"I'm Sam. I live here" as I pointed toward my house.

"I'm Craig. This is my dog Golden Boy." The dog was already sniffing my crotch and wagging its tail. As I sized up the boy, I realized he was a golden boy as well. He had a sleeveless tank and a pair of army fatigue pants on. His boots were military boots. He had a head of blonde hair, easily tousled when the wind blew.

"Where are you from, Craig?" The fact that I was in a Leather jock and chaps didn't seem to bother him.

"Oh, I live about half a mile downstream. I've seen you out in your yard cutting grass."

"Yeah, it needs to be done every so often, doesn't it?"

"Yes, Sir," was his reply.

"You want to come up and share a smoke?"

"Sure," Craig answered as he started up the bank of the creek. I gave him a hand up. His arms were muscular and his pecs flexed as he took my hand.

There was no way for me to avoid showing my ass to him as we marched across the backyard. He tied Golden Boy to the fence and we settled in the chairs on the back porch. My humidor was left there from the session with the D.C. boy and so, I offered Craig a cigar.

He clipped it and pulled out a lighter from his pants pocket. His belly was trim and I could now see a nice, long dick in his pants.

We traded work information as well as his background. He was an easygoing boy and I knew he was interested as he continued to rub his chest and crotch area.

"Why don't you take off your pants? They are soaked at the bottom. Put them over the porch rail, let them dry."

He stood up and quickly shed the pants, revealing a filled Leather jock.

"Leather, huh?" as I playfully tweaked his bulging cod.

"Yes, Sir. I was so hoping you'd be out here this afternoon. I've waded that stream more than once, Sir, hoping to get a glimpse of you."

"Oh?" I questioned.

"Yes, Sir. I've walked by with Golden Boy when you've been cutting your grass – always in your Leathers."

It was true, I loved to sweat in Leather and accomplished a lot of my yardwork in my old, comfortable Leathers.

"Why didn't you stop, son?"

"Oh, I was much too intimidated..."

I laughed and gave him a friendly slap on the shoulder and drew his handsome face to mine. We engaged in a long, tongued kiss.

"Want to come in and see my Leather art collection?" God, was I the original dirty old man, asking a boy to see my etchings.

I didn't have to ask him twice as he stood up and we went inside.

I guided him through the collection of homoerotic art that graced the walls of my house. "The best is upstairs..." as I led the way up the staircase. My favorite, a picture of my spiked Leather cod bulging with my cock was above the fireplace in the bedroom. When the boy saw this, he dropped to his knees and begged, "Please let me taste your cock, Sir."

Now how could I deny a boy a simple request?

I pulled my jock aside, and my cock sprang forth.

The boy guided it into his eager mouth and he sucked me expertly.

Afterward, we lay in each other's arms in my bed just long enough for my S&M tendencies to kick in.

"How about trying this on?" I said, as I handed him my Leather smokehood. It was laying on the bureau, left there after my play session with the D.C. sub.

He placed it over his face and I laced it tightly into place.

Damn, he looked attractive. A nice muscular body with just a hood and a jock. Fine blond hair covering his body, including what I assumed was a healthy bush around his cock and balls. I would know soon enough. As I threw on my motorcycle jacket, I asked him to put his boots back on and led him into the basement. He held up his wrists as I placed a pair of tight Leather cuffs around each one and padlocked them to the chains on the dungeon wall.

I oiled up a dildo and maneuvered it up his tender ass. His body arched upward as the substitute cock made its way up his boyhole. He didn't complain.

"Hold it in there, boy," I warned him as his asscheeks squeezed tightly around the top of the dildo.

I picked up my favorite flogger and began a slow rotation of flogs across his back and asscheeks. The boy was straining to keep his ass tight while receiving the floggings.

I chuckled as I saw him wince as the floggings became more intense.

I was a sadomasochist after all and liked to see a boy take his Leatherman's beatings.

The floggings continued and the boy's head arched upward as he tried unsuccessfully to keep the dildo up his ass.

It slipped out.

"Now, you'll have to pay for that transgression, son," I calmly said, as I greased my own pole and slowly inserted it up his hole, discarding the dildo on the basement floor.

"This one will stay in place, boy."

I continued the assault on his shoulders and ribcage with a small cat-o-nine-tails. That fucker could be intense as the Leather tails marked my floggings. The boy's head was writhing from side to side as the lashings intensified. My cock was fully inserted in his boyhole, throbbing with the intensity of excitement when it reaches near climax. The boy's arms were now straining against the chains which held him firmly to the dungeon wall.

His asscheeks flexed tightly, holding my cock captive. A delicious feeling.

I crushed my Leathered body against his naked skin. The boy let out a long sigh, his head arching upward. I looked and his cock was totally aroused, jutting out of the top of his jockstrap. His cock pressed against the stone wall. I reached around, pulling his throbbing meat out of the jockstrap and grasped it firmly in my Leathered hands.

As if twisting in the wind, or dancing an intense, sexual dance, we moved in one rhythm – my cock pounding into his boyhole, my hand squeezing his throbbing cock. His body responding to the movement of my cock – his back arching, his arms twisting and turning within the chained confines. We continued for only a short time before both our heads arched backward and I pumped a load up his ass and he shot a load against the wall. We both yelled 'Fuck' simultaneously and I collapsed against his body, crushing his spent dick against the wall.

I released the boy from his wrist restraints and he fell to his knees. He began swabbing my cockhead with his grateful tongue.

Lest you think the day was over, I led the boy, with dripping cock, to the toolshed where my workover table was situated. We checked on his dog Golden Boy and found him peacefully sleeping. I led my own golden boy to the toolshed.

The boy relaxed as I placed boot restraints around each booted foot and elevated his feet into the chains suspended at the end of the table. His wrists were once again placed in wrist restraints and those were secured to chains at the other end of the table. I methodically placed bondage ropes around his chest, secured them tightly to either side of the table with large steel rings. The boy was trussed into place – he wasn't going anywhere. I stepped back to observe the bondage boy. Something was missing... aah, yes, heavy gator clamps attached to his unsuspecting nips. His head shook from side to side as the clamps pinched into his boynips.

"You'll get used to them, son," I assured him.

His only response was a deep moan as he accustomed himself to his new situation.

I removed my jacket and placed a pair of clamps on my own nips.

I leaned over him and pulled on the chain short wiring his nips to my sadistic pleasures.

He moaned deeply again.

With the chain from his clamps wrapped around my right hand, I began paddling his stomach and elevated ass with a small Leather paddle. The whack of the paddle, despite any pain it inflicted, caused his cock to rise once again.

I could feel my own cock rising.

I crawled on top of the boy, until our dicks were rubbing against one another's. I began a slow, rhythmic rubbing of our bodies against one another. Laying down on him, crushing our clamped tits against one another's. My hands pulling his hooded face toward mine. Our tongues deep into each other's mouths. I could feel both our cocks pulsating, enjoying the heat of one another's bodies. His arms were straining against the chained wrist restraints. The mirror at the end of the table was in perfect position for me to look up and see me on top of the boy. It was almost as if there were another Daddy and his boy in the room. My cock got even harder, watching my Leathered body gliding back and forth on top of the willing boy. My Leathered arms rubbing his bound arms and chest. The boy's arms straining against the chains.

Watching myself in the mirror was a tremendous turn on for my cock as well as the handsome young man beneath me.

I wanted to fuck this boy with passion. I maneuvered myself off the table and unchained his legs. I pulled him down toward the end of the table, fully extending his arms above his head. I placed several large blocks of wood on the floor and standing on them was now dick-level with his boyhole.

I slung his feet and legs over my shoulders.

Spitting on my gloved hand, I lubed up my glove and went exploring.

First one, then three fingers, were inserted. Finally, my whole fist was up the boy's ass. He flinched and twisted, screamed as my fist moved up his ass.

All the while, I was talking him through it. Talking in quiet, confident tones that he was in his Master's care and that I wouldn't let anything happen to him. He seemed to relax a little and his ass accepted my fist more readily.

Once I loosened his hole, I pulled out my fist and inserted my manrod.

I began a slow, relaxed pumping, holding on to his thighs as my cock slid in and out. The boy seemed much more at ease and was not straining against the chains. His head occasionally rolled from side to side, but from his body posture you could tell he was enjoying it.

Fuck, it felt so good. Pumping my cock in this beautiful boy's ass which was covered in a fine golden fur. I rubbed his thighs, his flat stomach, his calves with my gloved hands... I continued the gentle gliding in and out of that golden ass until my dick was fully engorged. I couldn't help my sadistic streak surfacing as I became more fully aroused. My pumping intensified. I gripped his asscheeks more firmly. I slapped them with my gloved hands. My cock wanted to explore the boy's ass further as I thrust my cock in and out, seeming to dig deeper each time. The boy began moaning, panting, rolling his head from side to side.

All that was missing was background music gathering force to a final crescendo of a man and his boy fucking.

I was unrelenting as I continued my assault on that boy's virgin hole. I wanted to plant my seed in that boy's golden ass. As I continued to pump, I slapped his asscheeks with more force. I reached up and slapped his flat stomach. I pulled his legs and arms in a vertical position and increased the frenzy of my pumping action.

The boy moaned, his head writhing from side to side. He was screaming, but the hood muffled his pleas.

I wouldn't have stopped. My cock was swollen to its maximum capacity inside the boy's hole and I aimed to shoot my cum.

Fuck, it felt so good as I increased the intensity of fucking. I was sweating, the sweat dripping off my forehead and chest on to the boy's asscheeks. I began a barrage of hard slaps against that boy's golden asscheeks. Pumping.

Fucking. Sweating.

"FUCK!" I yelled as my cock released a massive load of cum up that boy's golden chute. It seemed like an inexhaustible supply of cum as I kept ejaculating.

I was sweating and panting. My knees seemed to buckle. It was one of the best fucks of my life.

I have since adopted Golden Boy. He's a good boy. Oh, yeah, and his dog has come to live with us too.

WHO'S YOUR DADDY?

Steve and I had flirted with each other on an internet chatroom for more than a year until we finally met up at the Cellblock in Chicago during the International Mr. Leather contest.

We were brothers under the black skins which we both wore on a daily basis. The question remained, however, "Who was the bigger Leatherman?" We both vied for the position of top during our internet conversations which were both raunchy and passionate, calling each other 'boy' during our conversations and telling each other what we would do to one another until one relented and became the submissive in actual play sessions. He is more muscular than me, no doubt about it. But, I can be like a wiry pit bull when pressed.

"I'll meet you in the lobby during IML on Saturday night..." Steve wrote before we both realized that there would be hundreds of Leather-clad men in attendance. The likelihood of hooking up with one guy that you had chatted with was remote. I stood in the lobby for forty-five minutes or so before the ass of a cute

Canadian caught my eye and we were soon up in my fifteenth floor room, um... playing. Steve would have to wait.

Later, after the cute Canadian ass had been reddened by the flogger and paddle on my belt and I had satisfied my manly desires I traveled to the Cellblock. At first it was pretty dismal but by and by, I began to chat with other handsome Leathermen and Steve was temporarily forgotten. I was chatting with an attractive Englishman in the front of the bar, when a handsome man, dressed in full black Leathers, sailed into the bar.

"Steve?" I wondered. I just couldn't quite tell. Every time I would maneuver to get a better look, the crowd would swallow him up and I would resume my conversation with the English bloke. Finally, the Leather gods looked kindly upon me and the handsome man sauntered toward the bar to order another drink.

I grabbed his left arm and said "Are you Steve?"

He looked at me, assessing me, and replied, "If you want me to be..."

"No, it's me, Samuel."

He removed his mirrored sunglasses, "Damned, if it isn't."

For the next twenty minutes, the bar ceased to exist – we were locked into a deep throated kiss, our codpieces pressed into one another's. My cock was so hard, pressing against this masculine specimen of Leatherhood and apparently, I had the same effect on his cock.

Our immediate thoughts were to go back to my room at the Hotel. Well, we waited for the damned bus so long that both of our cocks had shrunk from no use and so, the mission was aborted. Our rockets had misfired, so to speak.

A week or so later, we had both returned to our respective homes and continued the horny sex talk over the internet.

Steve is retired, I'm still working. I encouraged him to make a visit on his Harley which was so prominently displayed in his photos. That's cleaning up the dialogue, which said in part "Drag your mangy ass to Pennsylvania, bitch boy..."

About two weeks later, I was relaxing in my Leathers, out in my hammock. It was a beautiful, sunny day and my cock was hardened both by the sun and by the porn I was looking at. I puffed on a big cigar.

I had spent the morning gardening in Leather and so was covered in a layer of grime, my boots were blotched with mud, and I exuded a strong smell of mansweat.

Without warning, a Harley pulled into the yard. Thinking it was one of my boys, I stood up and viewed a man in full black Leather, mirrored sunglasses, and a stride of confidence as he marched toward me. This was no boy – not yet, anyway.

"Hey, you fucker..." as I slapped Steve on the back and we embraced one another.

With that, the fucker threw me to the ground, tore off my cod, and was squeezing my cock and balls in a vice-like grip. It did catch me momentarily off guard as I attempted to gain control. His fucking hands seemed to be everywhere at once.

"I've been on my cycle for close to twelve straight hours," Steve said in between gropings, "and I aim to get what I came for, pussy boy."

"You came to the wrong place then, bitch..." as I succeeded in rolling him over and flattening him against the ground.

We wrestled around on the ground, both of us tearing at each other like wild animals.

Soon Steve's jacket was off, revealing his two handsome mounds of titflesh. I squeezed them hard.

"These are mine, bitch boy..."

"I'm taking them back" as he punched me with both gloved hands in the chest, pushing me backward. Within seconds he was on top of me once again. As I fell backward, however, my right hand landed near his cod. I ripped the cod off and was holding onto his mancock. I squeezed with all my might.

"Aaahh," he exclaimed. It seemed to drain some of his power and energy and I took advantage of it. I lunged forward and had him on his back once again, never releasing his cock. I mounted his torso, my right hand in a backward position.

We were both sweating, heaving from exertion. I raised his head off the ground with my gloved left hand and looked him straight in his eyes. "Say, Uncle Fucker before I release your cock."

"Fuck you," he replied and with that, he started bucking like a bronco. I felt like a rodeo rider, holding onto that saddle horn for dear life. He continued to buck, until I felt a large spray of cum. With that, a generous load followed. It made his cock slippery and harder to hold onto. But I was determined....

Finally he conceded. "Okay, I was the first to shoot, you win this round, you mutha fucker."

With that he lay quietly, still heaving.

I unsnapped my cod and my swollen cock sprang forth. I sat on his chest and directed my cock toward his mouth.

"Suck me, you bitch boy" as I inserted my cock in his mouth. True to his word, he opened his mouth wide and gave me one of the best blow jobs I've ever had.

I was so close to the edge that it took me only a couple of minutes to shoot a load.

After that, we lay on the grass – dirty, sweaty, and enjoying each other's homomasculine company. We kissed long and hard, pulling on each other's tongues. The smell of our mutual Leathers mixed with our mansweat and manjuice was overpowering. In just a few minutes, both our cocks had recovered and were pressed against one another's. I slipped down between his legs and worshipped his cock and bullballs. I sucked on his pole, tonguing his pisshole. The world ceased to exist as I reached up and caressed his muscled stomach, occasionally tweaking his mantits. He lay with his back arched and his eyes closed. At this point, I just wanted that handsome cock in my mouth for a very long time.

"Don't shoot, brother..." I thought silently.

I sucked on it longer and harder, it tasted so good.

I wasn't watching his face which was now constricted. He was apparently putting every effort into not shooting and prolonging the pleasure.

I began tonguing the very tip of his cock and Steve's face grimaced as he tried to hold in his cum. He started cursing, calling me every name under the sun. It was to no avail. For within seconds, his cockcream slid down my throat and I continuing tonguing his handsome pole until I tongued him dry.

"You fucker, I can usually control it..." he winced.

"Shows you who is the bigger Leatherman, bitch."

I climbed off him and offered him a hand up. Instead he pulled me on top of him and we explored each other's Leathered body some more.

By this time, the sun was sinking in the west. I invited him to my back porch for a drink. I knew his favorite drink was a gin and tonic and so, I made a whole batch.

We sat in our sweaty Leathers on the back porch for some time. I brought out my humidor and we each selected a big ringed cigar.

"You know, bro, smoking makes me horny," Steve said, "it reminds me I should have a big cock in my mouth."

I was stroking my cod and was certainly willing to accommodate his wish. I straddled his chair and ripped off my cod. My dick arched upward. Soon, it was pulsating in Steve's mouth. He had leaned back in his chair as I pumped my cock into the back of his throat. He could take it all. I cupped the back of his head with my gloved hands as I thrust it in as far as I could.

I squeezed my balls in between my thighs to prolong the sucking as he continued to vacuum my rod.

Just then I heard a cycle head down my driveway and I glanced over to see a boy I had played with on several occasions. Let's call him 'Dutch'. He was a muscle boy from the Netherlands.

Steve, who had his eyes closed, didn't seem to notice the cycle or the boy who was dismounting from the cycle.

And I sure as hell didn't want to Steve to stop.

The boy came up onto the porch with a grin on his face. I momentarily turned my attentions to Dutch, motioning for him to kneel on the porch, with his head below my crotch. He needed no further instruction as he pulled off Steve's cod and began sucking on Steve's enlarged cock, which had cum juice in the slit.

Steve, now aware of his cock being sucked!, only paused a second before resuming a second incredible blow job.

Dutch's head was bobbing up and down on Steve's cock, my balls were flapping over Dutch's head.

What a fucking erotic three-way! I couldn't contain myself any longer and shot. Within seconds, Steve erupted in Dutch's mouth.

Steve continued to lap up my juice while Dutch performed the same clean-up operation on Steve.

Dutch dutifully assumed the 'table' position and Steve and I propped our booted feet on his back. We pulled out cigars.

"I should give Dutch one too." as I reached to open the humidor. "Oh, wait, something's missing..." as I left the porch. I disappeared inside and brought back my Leather hood. With that tightly laced into place on Dutch's head, I then gave him a cigar to smoke as well.

I wish I could paint a picture of the scene. Our booted feet propped on the back of a muscular Leather boy. He was smoking silently as Steve and I continued our raunchy conversation. We pulled on each other's cocks as we continued the conversation. Dutch's cock and balls received the attention of our gloved hands, you can be assured. Over the next twenty-four hours, we worked over Dutch in this continuous Leathersex session – flogging, fucking, fisting – the three f's of sadomasochism.

He responded well. And, of course, Steve and I continued fucking one another during his visit.

Damn, it was a visit none of us will soon forget. By the time of Steve's next visit, both our cocks may have recovered, but they will never be the same. And who is the bigger Leatherman? Hell, it's me. Let Steve write his own version of the story.

TENDERIZING

From all accounts, the boy was worth traveling for. We had met on a website. I usually insist that boys come to me. After all, my toolshed and dungeon were not transportable. But I had chatted with him at length, outlining my expectations, and he seemed eager and responsive to my demands. He appeared to be a worthy candidate. I'd beat his ass if he was and for that matter, if he wasn't.

I packed up my toolbag before I left for work that morning. Checked my selection of floggers and paddles, a Leather hood, wrist and ankle restraints, and bondage rope. For once, my miserable white collar desk job went swiftly and I was soon back home. I quickly stripped out of my white collar suit and tie and began the transformation into a sadistic Leatherman. Tight harness, cod pants with the spiked cod, Wescos to the crotch, and my oldest, most comfortable cycle jacket. Cigar pouch in the pocket. My Muir cap was placed reverently in my tool bag. Damascus gloves were the final touch before loading my gear onto my Harley. With my helmet in place, I exited for my night of play.

I had memorized the instructions to the boy's house and was there ahead of schedule. The house was in a toney neighborhood outside of Baltimore. A manicured lawn – even the American flag was flying proudly outside of the house which looked like it contained a typical American family. I expected a golden retriever to come bounding out of the house as I rang the doorbell.

Instead the door swung open to reveal a boy in Leather collar and jock. He knelt as I entered the house.

"Good afternoon, Sir. It is my pleasure to have you here..."

I took in his handsome features. He was a good-looking masculine boy. Black hair, shortly cropped. Clean-shaven. A fair amount of black fur on his chest with two rosy nips rising from muscular pecs. A line of fur ran down and disappeared into the Leather jock. He was barefoot.

"Good afternoon, boy. Lick your man's boots in appreciation for me being here."

I stood framed in the open doorway as he complied with my command.

He fondled the heel of the boot as he lay on the floor and gave my boots a good tongue-worshipping. I extracted one of my floggers from my toolbag and gave him a few lashes across the back. He flinched as each strike hit his back but it did not stop him from his mission. He massaged my booted feet as he continued to lick the boots to an even shine.

"Good boy," I replied as he continued to service my boots.

His ass was arched in the air as he licked the heels. I gave it a few good whacks with the flogger.

Once he had finished the base of the boots, I caught his jaw and indicated that I wanted him to lick the rest of the boot. He squatted as he worked his way up the crotch-length boots.

Tonguing every inch, massaging with his hands as he went. My cock rose in my cod as he continued the servicing.

"Good boy. Lick that cod – I want to feel your tongue through the Leather separating my cock from your tongue."

The boy began a more vigorous tonguing, stopping only to juice up his mouth with more spit. I could feel his tongue, concentrating on the head of my cock. I intensified the flogging on his ass.

His ass flinched as the strips of black Leather landed with a crack.

His arms encircled my ass as he continued to press into my codpiece with his tongue.

I encouraged him to continue, my cod was shining from the licking.

"Pull the cod off slowly, one snap at a time with your teeth, boy," I instructed.

He did that with some effort, but soon my bulging manrod was standing erect in front of his willing mouth.

"Suck my dick, boy."

He needed no prompting as his mouth swallowed my cock. It felt delicious.

The boy moaned as his eager mouth took in the head and shaft of my swollen cock.

My back arched as I pressed the cock into the back of his mouth. I pulled his head forward until my cock was fully in his mouth. As I began to slowly pump my cock in and out, I continued to flog his back and ass with my flogger. He twitched and flinched, but it did not interrupt his duties.

I began a frenzied pumping as my cock prepared for an explosion of cum in the willing boy's mouth.

The boy could sense the moment was near and began vacuuming the cockhead.

I fucked that boy's mouth with my cock and soon shot a load of jism down his throat. The cum spurted out of his mouth and down his chest.

"Fuck!" I yelled as I came. The boy continued vacuuming until he had sucked the cock dry.

With that, he withdrew his mouth. "May I lick the cum off my chest, Sir?" he asked.

"Yes, boy. Make sure you don't miss a drop." I replied. He willingly complied to my command, licking each finger as he swabbed it up. His cock was arched and straining against his jockstrap.

He tentatively reached down to touch his extended cock, but I pushed it away.

"You won't touch your cock, and you won't cum, until I tell you to, boy."

A moment of unwillingness flashed across his face, but I smacked him across the cheek with my gloved hand.

"You will obey what I say, boy. Where do you have our set-up, boy?"

"Down in the basement, Sir."

"On your feet, boy."

When he hesitated, I grabbed him under the jaw and pulled him to his feet.

"Down to the basement, boy."

I led him down the flight of steps to a workbench which had been cleared of his tools – they were piled neatly on a set of nearby shelves.

"On the table, boy. Face down."

He climbed onto the table and spread himself on the table. His feet overlapped over the end of the table.

I quickly handcuffed his arms above his head and placed a pair of ankle restraints on his feet. A separating bar, attached to the ankle restraints, was placed between them.

I tied his wrists closely together with bondage rope and anchored the rope to a nearby support beam. Similarly, the ankles were tied off to another support beam. I then hooded him with a padded Leather hood

With the boy trussed into place, I pulled out my selection of paddles and remaining floggers.

I quietly explained to him the rotation of flogs and paddles that I was about to execute on his ass and back.

He nodded his head in reply. I placed a ballgag in his mouth in case he was a screamer.

With that, the tenderizing of the boyflesh began.

I was gentle with the first rotation and he seemed to respond well. The subsequent rotations, of course, increased in intensity. He flinched and moaned, and his ass and back reddened considerably. I rubbed his body in between rotations and made sure that he was all right.

It was then that my mean streak took over and I began a more intensified flogging. His ass and back were flinching as I inflicted a higher level of pain. Damn, it felt good to have this boy under my control. I wanted him to feel the full fury of my flogging. And he did. He twisted and jerked as I struck him again and again. I occasionally reached down to stroke my cock which was bulging in its Leather cod. I unsnapped the cod and my cock sprang forth like a fucking copperhead. Its venomous cum was sparkling in the dim light of the basement.

I marched around and jerked the boy's head up, making eye contact.

"You like it, boy?" I removed the ballgag so he could reply.

The boy hesitantly said, "Yes, Sir."

"You'll like this too..." and with that I thrust my throbbing manmeat into his mouth.

He began to choke and gag.

I struck his back several times with my flogger, "You'll take it like the meat slut I want you to be."

I pushed it more forcibly into his mouth. His throat began to relax and he began sucking on my mancock with the servicing he knew he had to provide in order to satisfy my Leather desires.

I pumped my cock in and out of his mouth. He began to relax and enjoy it. Moaning softly as he sucked.

As I reached climax, I arched my back and shot a cumload down his throat. The cum dribbled down his Leathered chin.

My cock remained in his mouth for some time as it softened. Damn, it felt good.

We were not through, however. I marched around to the side of the table and began flogging him once again.

The boy twisted and moaned. I noticed that he was arching his back to receive the floggings. I could see now that his cock was fully aroused, pressing against the table.

I marched around to the head of the table and roughly lifted his head. I got right down into his face, and shouted "THAT DICK OF YOURS IS MINE – DON'T YOU SHOOT OR THERE WILL BE HELL TO PAY – YOU SHOOT AT MY COMMAND, BOY." The boy whimpered as I removed his gag once more.

"Sir... I can't control it, Sir. I've never been with a man like you before. I'm so totally..."

"Shut the fuck up. You heard me... control it. Do whatever it takes...."

I returned to lashing his ass with my flogger. His ass was crisscrossed with red marks, a few drops of blood made their appearance with this last lashing.

Even though I wanted to continue, I marched upstairs and found some alcohol and a towel to clean the areas.

As I returned to the basement, the boy was rubbing his cock against the table, groaning as he attempted to jack off.

"WHAT DID I TELL YOU, BOY?"

I smacked him. I smacked him hard across the cheek with my gloved hand.

The boy whimpered as I toweled the blood off his ass.

I removed his fetters, but placed him with his back down on the table. I reshackled him. His cock was hard and erect and pre-cum was oozing out of his piss slit. His attempts at self-gratification had massaged the cock out of the Leather jockstrap.

"Don't you cum, boy, you heard me..."

The boy's facial muscles tightened under the hood as he attempted to hold in the cock's juices. It was no use. The boy's cock shot a load of cum skyward, landing on his chest.

I mopped up the cum with the towel and smeared it on the hood, tantalizingly close to his lips. Not close enough to his lips, however. He wouldn't have the pleasure of licking it off of his hooded face until ordered to do so.

"Boys need to be punished when they disobey this Leatherman."

With that, I let loose a series of floggings across his chest, making sure I connected the Leather straps with his nips. He yelled in pain. I shoved the ballgag in his mouth.

With my Leather gloved hands. I twisted on those nipples until he was jerking from side to side. His head was shaking "NO" as he attempted to scream. Sadist that I am, it only made me pull and twist harder.

I reached down and pulled on his balls. That extracted another attempted scream.

I worked over that boy's cock and balls with my gloved hands in a vicelike grip. The boy was letting forth with a protracted scream, muffled by the ball gag.

I don't know how long we went at it, but it was a good, long session.

My cock, of course, was fully aroused. I climbed on the table and sat on the boy's chest. I unsnapped my cod and my cock smacked him in the face. I once again inserted my manrod into his mouth and pumped a third load of jism down his throat. This action calmed the boy.

After a prolonged session, I finally released the boy from the workover table.

He looked dazed and fully submissive as I escorted him off the table.

He dropped to his knees and began licking my boots which had accumulated dirt and dust from the basement, as well as some drops of cum. I made him lick the dried cum off of my hood once I removed it from his head.

"Thank you, Master," he quietly said.

I silently packed up my gear and headed to the basement door.

"When will you be back, Sir?"

I turned and said, "I don't know, boy, but be ready for me when I come."

"Yes, Sir," he replied as I closed the door.

Yes, the trip to Baltimore was well worth it. He needed my discipline but I think with my supervision and training he will turn into a good fuckboy. It is now two weeks later and I am just pulling into the driveway of the house with the well-manicured lawn. Hope the boy is home. I have a few more toys guaranteed to tenderize the boy.

WELCOME TO
THE BROTHERHOOD

The Leatherman's directions had been very explicit, replying to the internet search of the candidate. "Take Route 514 until you reach Shade Lane. The "h" of the word "Shade" is disintegrating and so, it looks like SADE Lane. Turn left. Follow that lane for 1.3 miles. There will be a dirt lane off to the right. It is somewhat hard to find because it is obscured by overhanging trees. Find the dirt lane and follow it for 2.4 miles until you reach a farmhouse. The farmhouse is painted white and has a stone foundation. I will meet you at this location."

The boy was also told to arrive in blue jeans, boots, and a plain white tee shirt.

The boy drove his car slowly and still missed the exit off of Shade Lane. He turned around and crept slowly back until he found the obscured lane. As he entered the dirt lane he wondered aloud, "Should I be doing this? This is a little scary..." Still the intriguing notion of being with a real Leatherman was ingrained in his fantasy life and despite his trepidation he drove down the dirt lane. The day was evaporating and it would soon be dark. What would greet him at the end of the lane, the boy wondered.

A farmhouse slowly emerged from the surrounding wilderness. As he drove into the yard, he could see the shape of outbuildings and a farmhouse lighted with electric lights. "Well, at least it looks pleasant." The house needed a good coat of paint, but it was surrounded with flower bushes and a large vegetable garden off to one side. He parked his car and emerged from the car.

He looked nervously around as he climbed the steps to the back porch. He knocked on the door.

"Down here" a voice called.

He ascended the steps only to find a figure standing next to a set of basement steps.

As the boy approached, he took in as many details as he could. The figure was dressed in head-to-toe black Leather. His head was covered in a black Leather hood, revealing only his eyes and a lighted cigar emerging from the hole cut out for the mouth.

"I am the guardian of the portals of Leather. Who seeks entrance?"

"Shit," the boy thought, "I feel like I'm in some cheesy B movie," but he responded, "It's me, Rod...I answered your email..."

The Leatherman approached the boy. He was a large, muscular man. He wore a motorcycle jacket with heavy chains on both the epaulets. His hands were covered in heavy motorcycle gauntlets. He wore black Leather pants with a chain mail codpiece. His boots were buckled at the knees.

"How do you do, Sir," the boy answered somewhat tremulously and he tentatively stuck out his hand to shake that of the Leatherman.

The man stuck his hand out in greeting and as Rod gripped the man's hand, his hand was wrenched behind his back. A Leather wrist restraint was soon in place.

Before Rod could protest, the Leatherman had thrown him roughly to the ground and a Leathered knee was placed squarely in the boy's crotch.

"You were fifteen minutes late, asshole – I'm not used to waiting for a piece of shit like you."

With that the Leatherman backhanded the boy's face and despite the boy's resolve to be a man about this encounter, tears came to his eyes.

"I'm sorry, Sir, I got lost..." the boy sputtered.

"You'll be even more damned sorry before this session is over..."

The Leatherman placed a Leather wrist restraint around the boy's other wrist, locked the two into place and dragged the boy up to his feet with the waist of his jeans.

He dragged the struggling boy down the basement steps. They entered a room with no light. The boy was unceremoniously thrown onto a table which was padded with a thickened layer of foam and covered in rubber sheeting. His arms were quickly refastened above his head, attached to a heavy metal chain. As the boy's eyes grew accustomed to the darkness, he viewed a wall of paddles, whips and chains.

It was then that a glaring white light was turned on, revealing the magnificence of the black-skin clad Leatherman. Despite his fear, Rod was excited. Never had he viewed a more magnificent specimen of manhood. He trembled with anticipation of the night ahead.

"Let's take a look at you," the Leatherman remarked as he pulled a small knife from his belt.

With that he cut Rod's tee shirt off his chest. Rod had a nicely defined chest and he was proud of it. His pecs were firm and his nipples had rings in them. The Leatherman seemed to smile an appreciative smile behind the Leathered hood. "Nice chest, boy."

Rod began to warm to the scene and thanked his Leatherman for the compliment, "I work out, Sir, to please a man like you..."

"Oh, you do, do you, boy?" With that he took his lighted cigar to one of the tit rings. As it heated the metal, the searing burn transferred to the boy's tits. "AAAHHH" he screamed. For the second time, the Leatherman slapped him roughly with his gauntleted hand. The surprised look on the boy's face was met with a laugh. The man's eyes which were piercing blue behind the hood, remained unblinking.

"That's just a taste of what is to come..."

"Please, Leatherman, Sir, let me show you what a good boy I can be, I love to service cock."

"You'll do that when I tell you to, asshole."

For the next twenty minutes or so, the boy's nips were subjected to the heat of the Leatherman's cigar. The Leatherman was obviously enjoying this episode quite a bit. The boy was astonished when the man unzipped his own jacket and proceeded to apply the cigar to his own massive nipple rings. The man held the cigar to his own rings for a longer time than the boy could imagine any human could endure. All the while, the man's ice blue eyes were unblinking, but a groan of pleasure had emerged from the Leatherman.

"I seldom subject one of my boys to anything which I myself don't enjoy..."

The Leatherman's gauntleted hands began rubbing the boy's chest. The feel of the soft, buttery Leather had its effect on the boy and soon his cock had hardened to a mound within his blue jeans.

The Leatherman removed his right gauntlet to reveal a skin-tight Leather glove. The man reached down and grabbed the boy's cock and balls through the boy's faded jeans. His iron grip softened the boy's cock and made it want to retreat up to his throat. The man removed the other gauntlet and worked the jeans down around the boys' ankles. A Leather cockring encircled the boy's dick and balls. His balls were nice and tight and the cock had retreated but the Leatherman began massaging the cock head and shaft and soon the boy was nice and firm again.

The Leatherman retreated to the wall of whips and chose a small cat-of-nine-tails. He was massaging his cock through his chain mail cod and the boy could see that the man's cock was beautiful. It looked as if it were sculpted of marble, the veins standing out along the shaft and a nice mushroom head topping that.

Despite the warning in his head that the Leatherman was the one in control, the boy suggested, "Please, sir, I want to take your cock in my mouth..."

The cat of nine tails struck him across the face, leaving a reddened mark that the boy would not soon forget. For the next half hour, the boy was repeatedly struck with the whip, across his sensitive balls, his chest, and his face. His cock received extended treatment from the whip and despite the lashings, he hardened. He watched the Leatherman's hooded face, but no emotion registered as the Leatherman concentrated on the task at hand. Lashing after lashing and the Leatherman seemed to have worked himself into a frenzy.

The Leatherman's cock was outlined within the chain mail and seemed to pulse with the same energy. Energy that prompted him to continue into the night.

The boy's body ached from the repeated lashings and he began to writhe from side to side when the pain seemed that he could take it no more.

"STOP!" the boy yelled and he struggled to loose himself from the chained restraints that kept him tied to the table.

The man just laughed and his blue eyes stared the boy down.

"You'll take it until I want to stop."

With that, the Leatherman unsnapped his codpiece and his own manhood sprang forth. The man repeatedly lashed his own cock with the whip. The man was enjoying his own beatings and seems to have forgotten the boy. His back arched as the whip repeatedly struck his own manrod.

The boy was entranced by the Leatherman's cock. It arched upward and seemed to enlarge with each beating. Despite his fear, the boy begged the Leatherman to let him take part in the activity of pleasing his newly-found Leatherdaddy.

With that, the Leatherman replaced the cat-of-nine tails whip on the wall. He spring vaulted onto the table and was soon sitting on the boy's chest. His engorged dick was unceremoniously thrust into the boy's willing mouth. The boy gagged with the mancock in his throat, but he started sucking greedily. This was the best cock he had ever had the pleasure of servicing.

He was going to enjoy it, even if he couldn't breathe.

He focused briefly on the blue eyes behind the mask – they were cold and unblinking. However, a chuckle emerged from behind the mask. "Enjoying it, boy?" the Leatherman asked, "I knew you would, all the boys have..."

With that, the Leatherman shot a load of cum down the boy's throat. The boy gagged and gasped for breath. He felt his head being lifted and the cum slid more easily down his throat. He felt his nostrils being pinched shut and then he lost consciousness.

Sometime later, the boy awoke. He could not see anything. He realized that he was now laying with his chest on the table.

He realized pretty quickly that his head was encased in a black Leather hood and his hands were chained behind his back, restrained in Leather mitts. His ass was being paddled by several varieties of paddles, each more painful than the other.

The paddling was coming from four different directions.

As he tried to lift his head, a pair of forceful hands roughly pushed it down.

The boy lost consciousness once again. The paddlings continued.

When the boy woke once again, he was resting in a bed. No Leather restraints, no hood. His body ached, but in a delicious way. The boy opened his eyes only to view the Leathermaster standing at the foot of the bed. Standing on the left side were two hooded boys, their eyes unblinking from behind the hoods they wore. The boys were naked save for a jockstrap and hood they each wore. A similar boy was standing on the right.

"Well done, boy," the Leatherman commented, "you have done very well as an initiate. I would like you to become one of my boys."

The boy could only nod yes, as a Leather hood was placed over his head.

The Leatherman's expression changed to reveal a slight smile behind the hood. "Welcome to the Brother 'hood'."

A car, having missed the Shade Lane exit, turned around and crept slowly back, seeking the dirt lane.

THE HUSTLER

The young boy slouched seductively against the fencing. His elbows were propped on top of the fencing while his slender body arched outward. His rubber tank top revealed slender arms and a hairless upper chest. His slicked back hair and facial features prompted more than a few men to tell him that he looked like Leo DiCaprio. His blue jeans were well-worn and had a frayed hole near the tip of his cockhead. His right foot was crossed over his left foot, clad in scuffed harness boots. He dragged on a cigarette while he watched the endless variety of men pass him. Some ignored him, others gave him a once over, several stopped to say "Hello." The ones that stopped were usually middle-aged, balding, probably going home to wifey and the kids, but, having sized him up as a street hustler, approached him.

And that is what he was. Looking for the right trick. A quick blow job in the nearby alley. One hundred bucks. Hey, this was quality sucking. He was an excellent cocksucker.

It's not that he didn't have dreams and ambitions. When he wasn't sucking cock, he was painting. Big canvases, which weren't cheap. Studio space, not cheap. And his paintings were erotic, filled with naked men fornicating. If he liked a particular john, he would invite him to the studio and several had actually purchased paintings.

It was a dismal day for him. Not one $100 blow job and he had been standing here for close to two hours. He dragged on cigarette after cigarette, absently fondling his basket to attract interest.

He was eyeing a man, tall, slender, well-dressed, in suit and tie. The man's shoes were shined and he wore a pocket kerchief in his left breast pocket. As the man approached, Bryce attempted to make eye contact. The man seemed distracted by something or someone ahead of him on the street. Bryce didn't want to lose the possible eye contact, but he did glance the other way.

A Leatherman in full Leather regalia was hurrying down the street. Muir cap, heavy cycle jacket with cock rings on the right epaulet, harness, and a metal-studded cod on his black Leather pants. Knee-high boots. Bryce's cock hardened in his jeans. "Damn," he thought, "would I love to give him a cocksucking, I'd even do it for free."

Bryce glanced the other way, only to see the suited man standing near him. The man stood with feet apart and was pointing to the ground.

As the Leatherman approached, he knelt on the ground in front of the suited man, removed his hat, and bowed his head.

"Well, boi, you finally made it. You're late, you fuck-up..."

"I'm sorry, Sir," said the Leatherman in a soft voice, "the boi apologizes to Daddy for keeping him waiting." With that, the suited man slapped the Leatherman across the face.

"You'll get your ass whipped for this, boi."

Bryce was staring silently, having forgotten the lighted cigarette in his hand. As Bryce took it all in, he noticed that the pocket hanky was actually a black bandana. "S&M top," Bryce silently thought.

Bryce's dick got even harder. He wanted to see this scene of humiliation played out in its entirety. He hoped it would be right in front of him.

The suited man pointed to him, "You, boi, get your ass over here..."

Bryce pointed to himself and said, "Me? Sir..."

"I said NOW, boi."

Bryce hurried over to where the suited man and his Leatherboi were.

"You want to earn some extra money, boi?"

Bryce was apprehensive, but needed the money to pay his rent which had been overdue for a week.

"What do you have in mind, Sir? I charge a hundred bucks for a blow job."

"Just follow me and my boi..."

With that, the suit, followed by his Leatherboi and Bryce, walked a dozen blocks or so before entering an apartment at a fashionable address. The Leatherboi pressed the elevator button and stood aside to let his Master and Bryce step into the wallpapered exterior of the elevator.

As soon as the doors closed, the suit pushed his Leatherboi's head into his crotch.

"Worship my manhood, boi. In a few minutes you'll be servicing it. Right, boi?"

The Leatherboi only shook his head "Yes" as he buried his head into the man's pinstriped crotch.

Bryce looked on silently as the elevator finally reached its destination.

They entered an apartment with sleek black marble flooring, Leather furniture, and modern sculpture. Bryce's jaw dropped as he viewed the collection of artwork depicting men in various states of fucking.

The suit gruffly said to Bryce, "Look at it later, we have business to attend to."

He lead the two down a hallway and through two walnut paneled doors.

Bryce's jaw dropped for the second time as he viewed a playroom with mirrors, slings, paddles, whips, and other devices he could only imagine a function for.

The Leatherboi and the suit disappeared behind a closed door, leaving Bryce to examine the S&M toys a little more closely.

Within a few minutes, the suit had disappeared and the man was now in full, black Leather – head to toe. The silver on the beak of his cap and the metal-studded codpiece were gleaming as if shined before their use. His Leathers were oiled, including his tight black Leather gloves.

The Leatherboi entered the room. He was naked except for his knee-high boots. He positioned himself against a cross – a St. Andrew's cross (although Bryce didn't know it was called that). Cuffs were quickly placed around his wrists and ankles.

"You!" the man said to Bryce, "What's your name, son?"

"Bryce, Sir, but really, Sir... this looks like a private session....I really should leave...."

"You want to earn your money, now, don't you? Get me a cigar from the humidor over there and select one for yourself... I know you smoke, boi, I saw you smoking..."

Bryce obligingly retrieved two cigars and a lighter.

"You didn't clip it, son. A cigar needs to be punched or clipped. Get back over there and get a clip. It's on the table."

Bryce located the cigar clip and obligingly cut off the ends.

He handed the man a cigar and offered a light. The Daddy guided Bryce's hand to the cigar and held it there with his Leathered hand gripping Bryce's hand until his cigar had caught. The Leatherboi stood silently in his spread-eagled position while all this was transpiring.

The Daddy stoked his cigar for several minutes before selecting a broad Leather paddle off the wall.

"This is for being late..." the Daddy scolded the Leatherboi and proceeded to redden his boi's ass. The boi stood silently as he received his punishment.

110

Bryce's eyes widened as each smack of the paddle hit the boi's ass. He was increasingly afraid that he would be subjected to the same punishment.

"Sir... I really should go... "

The man turned to Bryce and growled, "You'll stay until I finish punishing my boi."

With that a barrage of paddlings continued until the boi was flinching with each whack of the paddle.

"Now, it's your turn, boi, paddle him." He motioned Bryce over to the cross.

"Sir, I really just like to suck cock..."

"I said NOW, boi" and the Leatherman grabbed Bryce's hand and placed the paddle in his right hand.

Bryce took several whacks of the paddle.

"More forcefully, boi. Are you a pansy-fucking ass?"

Bryce took several more whacks of the paddle, but the Leatherboi just stood calmly.

The Leatherman pressed his body against Bryce's back and guided the paddle as it smacked the asscheeks of the captive boi. The boi flinched this time.

The Leatherdaddy and Bryce remained in this intimate position. The Daddy's cod was pressed against the thin layer of denim of Bryce's jeans and Bryce could feel his own cock rising.

Once the Daddy was sufficiently impressed with Bryce's paddling, he pulled a heavy Leather flogger off the wall.

He began flogging his Leatherboi's back. Strike after strike until Bryce and he were alternating flogger and paddle.

The Leatherboi was moaning, his back arched and his muscled arms straining against the cuffs.

The session continued until the Leatherboi's back and ass were bright red. He was squeezing his eyes shut as the Leather toys continued their unceasing assault.

Bryce momentarily looked over and noticed that the man's bulge was huge. He could almost see the cock throbbing inside its Leather casing.

"Had enough, boi? You won't be late again, will you, boi?"

The Leatherboi answered in a quivering voice, "No, Sir."

The Leatherman released him from his restraints and ordered him on his knees.

"Unzip your pants, boi," the Leatherman ordered Bryce. Bryce, not sure what to expect now, slowly undid the jeans button and zipper. His pants dropped down around his boots. His cock was arching upward.

"boi, suck Bryce's cock."

The Leatherboi licked the piss slit of Bryce's cock. He then tongued the shaft and took Bryce's swollen cock in his mouth. Bryce's loose balls were soon tongued and joined Bryce's shaft in the Leatherboi's mouth. Bryce was moaning – in all the years he had sucked cock, it had rarely been reciprocated. Instinctively, he pulled the Leatherboi's head closer to swallow the entire package.

"Good boi," the Leatherman remarked as he smoked his cigar and fondled his own codpiece.

He reached over and fondled Bryce's asscheeks. The Leather gloves felt heavenly on Bryce's asscheeks and they began to relax. The Daddy's moved his gloved hand toward the boi's hole.

"Relax now, son" as the Daddy stuck first one, then three fingers up the hole.

Bryce, not expecting this intrusion, shot a load of cum into the Leatherboi's mouth. The Leatherboi tongued the remainder of cum off the cock shaft.

With the last drops of dew licked clean from his cock, Bryce made motions to leave.

"Not so fast, son. I want to see if you live up to your street reputation." The Leatherman pushed Bryce to his knees while unsnapping his cod. A handsome thick cock slapped Bryce on the cheek as it escaped its cod.

Bryce needed no second invitation. He began vacuuming the Daddy's cock with his cocksucking mouth. The Daddy rammed it further and further into Bryce's mouth. The Daddy pulled his Leatherboi toward him and began deep kissing his boi. The

Leatherboi responded – rubbing his Leatherman's pierced nips, shoulders, and the Dad's handsome Leather-covered ass. Bryce was sandwiched in between the two, a sea of Leather and male flesh surrounding him.

Bryce's mouth got a workout with the stud's cock in his mouth until the man could not control the release of his jism any longer. He shot a healthy stream of mancum down the hustler's throat. The boi continued to suck on it for some time, it tasted so good.

Once satisfied, the Leatherman pulled his cock out of the boi's throat.

"Now do my boi," the Leatherman ordered.

Bryce pivoted on his knees and faced the Leatherboi's erect dick, and positioned the cock in his willing mouth. He was a good cocksucker and edged the boi to ejaculation. Once there, he eased off, only to excite the boi's cock once again. After some time, however, Bryce silently wondered, "Why isn't he coming?"

As if reading Bryce's mind, the Leatherdaddy said, "He won't shoot until I order him to."

Finally with an order for cum release, the boi shot a healthy load into the hustler's mouth.

"Good bois," said the man as he fondled both of the bois' heads.

With the scene winding down, the Leatherman presented Bryce with five $100 bills, kept warm in the man's cod.

"Thank you, Sir."

"Get off the street, son," the Leatherman advised. Bryce explained that he was an artist, but hustling was more profitable.

The Leatherman was instrumental in getting Bryce an agent. His paintings now command high prices, but he continues to suck his Leatherman's cock and the cock of the Leatherboi. The three enjoy scenes similar to the one described above, often captured on canvas by Bryce and proudly displayed on the walls of the man's apartment.

THE PRIDE OF MANFUCKET

Tim O'Bryan walked down the series of piers to the clipper ship that would be his home for the next six months or so. He carried his meager possessions in a cloth bag that was hastily sewn by his widowed mother Caroline. Mrs. O'Bryan had six children and no income, and so, she was forced to consign Tim, her oldest boy, to a whaling ship. The O'Bryans had immigrated from Ireland just two years before, with hope in their hearts and very little else. Her husband John had died two months prior in a milling accident, leaving Mrs. O'Bryan destitute. Caroline had said her tearful goodbyes and the boy marched into the future not knowing when or if he would ever see his mother and family again.

The sailing ship looked both majestic and intimidating to the young boy, only sixteen. They had lied about his age, telling the coxswain that he was of the age of majority and worthy of sailing. Jones, the First Mate, was signing in the seamen as they arrived. *The Pride of Nantucket* was to set sail for a whaling expedition and would not return for at least six months.

O'Bryan was hustled to the lower deck and assigned a hammock in the most miserable section of the boat. It already smelled strongly of human excrement, mildew, and despite his best efforts, the boy gagged and like most other inexperienced seamen, made his way to the ship's rail to lose what little breakfast he had.

A muster was called before sunset and Tim stood among the seamen on the deck.

Within a few minutes of assembly, Captain Breckenridge made his appearance.

Tim's eyes beheld a handsome, tanned man of thirty-two. His hair was curly brown and his eyes matched the water of the Bay. He wore a waist-length navy blue jacket with handsome gold braiding that glistened in the sun, tight white Leather breeches and shined black Leather boots which terminated at the knee. Tight black Leather gloves covered the Captain's hands. Tim had never seen anyone so handsome.

"Gentlemen," the Captain bellowed, "I am Captain Breckenridge, the commander of *The Pride of Nantucket* and you are now my crew. I run an efficient ship and I tolerate no laxity in the conduct of my men." He ran through a whole litany of rules and regulations, but Tim barely heard the speech, so entranced was he by the handsome specimen of manhood. He noted every detail in his mind. As the Captain moved around the deck, Tim couldn't help but notice the glint of the sun on the braiding and the polished boots. The breeches were apparently of the finest tanned Leather and caressed the man's muscular thighs. His manhood was especially well-represented with a long, thick cock resting firmly down the left leg of the breeches. His ass was firm in the tightened breeches. Tim's own cock hardened but he disguised it with his crossed hands.

The ship set sail two mornings hence and Tim like many of the others spent a goodly portion of the time at the rail, wretching. The food was miserable, but the camaraderie and the lustiness of the men were soon appreciated by the recruit. They quickly accepted him as an affable, hardworking sort.

Jones, a pretty decent chap, took Tim under his wing and advised him on how to succeed while at sea, admonishing the boy to do whatever their Captain said.

Two weeks since setting sail, Tim was scrubbing the foredeck. He had adjusted well and was developing a trimness about him.

"Sailor, what is your name?"

Tim looked up from his work, only to discover the Captain standing in front of him.

Tim gulped, but hastened to his feet and saluted his Captain.

"Captain, Sir, O'Bryan, Sir."

'Carry on, son."

Tim dropped back to his knees and began scrubbing, but could not erase the image of the Captain standing above him.

That night, in his hammock, Tim couldn't stop recalling the details of the Captain. The long, hard cock was pressed against the Captain's left leg. The tall boots seemed to reach to the sky. Those buttery soft gloves caressing each of the Captain's strong fingers. Tim began playing with himself and began moaning softly.

"Tim, boy, ya thinking of a woman ya left behind..." joked Henderson in one of the adjoining hammocks.

"Sure he is, a handsome buck like him..." Hoban chimed in.

Pretty soon, the men surrounding Tim were taking bets on how long Tim would take to jack off, but Tim didn't even hear them. He was thinking of his Captain.

The next morning, Tim returned to his duties on deck. Good-natured taunting was heard from the men.

Tim was blushing with embarrassment when a pair of booted legs marched up to him.

The Captain stood before him once again and Tim hopped to his feet, saluting the Captain.

"Son, I want you to come to my cabin."

The boy followed the Captain, knowing that he was going to be reprimanded for his indecent actions of the night before. Someone had obviously been an informant to the Captain.

The Captain sat in his Leather upholstered chair and poured himself a glass of sherry. It would have been inappropriate for him to offer the boy a drink and so, he did not. Tim stood at attention, until the Captain indicated the boy should sit on a nearby bench.

"Son, what's your name again?"

"Timothy O'Bryan, Captain, Sir."

"Timothy, I have noticed that you are a hard worker, sober, good material for a sailor. On every trip, I usually promote one of my seamen to my cabin boy, to work as a personal assistant to me. Jones and I have conferred and we think you would be a good candidate for the position."

"Oh, yes Captain, Sir, I would like that very much, Sir."

"Fine, son. I will arrange for you to have the small antechamber within my quarters. First order of business, son, while I was out on inspection, that lout Carmichael slopped my boots full." The highly-shined boots indeed were stained. "Polish my boots, son."

The boy bent down and taking his own kerchief from around his neck, began to spit shine the left boot.

The Captain pressed the left boot against the boy's chest. The boy massaged his own spit into the boot Leather. Tim worked on it until the Captain gave the boy his nod of approval. Next, Tim concentrated on the right boot. Quick glances assured the boy that the Captain was pleased with his work as he smiled down at the boy several times. The Captain continued to sip his sherry and as he continued to relax he lighted a clay pipe which lay on a nearby table.

"Good work, son," the Captain commented. His left hand would occasionally rub his extended cock.

When the boots were completed, the Captain guided the boy's hand to the outline of the cock. The feeling of the soft Leather breeches hiding the man's massive cock was exciting the boy.

"Massage it, son."

"Captain, Sir?" the boy asked hesitantly.

"You heard me, boy, massage my cock. That's your Captain's orders."

The boy did not ask twice. He used both hands to fondle the length of the man's penis, covered in the white Leather.

The Captain unbuttoned his codpiece and the handsome cock was revealed.

It was tied into place down the left leg with a Leather strap. The strap was threaded through a gold ring which pierced the man's cockhead.

The boy gasped. He had never seen such a thing.

"Untie the strap, boy."

Tim hesitantly untied the strap and the man's mancock sprang forward.

"Suck my cock, boy." Tim entertained no thoughts of disobeying the Captain.

Tim inserted the cock's head and good portion of the shaft into his mouth and once he got used to it, began playfully tonguing the gold ring.

The Captain approved and using both Leather gloved hands, pushed the boy's head down further so that the boy could lick the Captain's balls.

As the Captain continued to relax, he unbuttoned his jacket. His chest was tanned from exposure to the sun and the boy was startled to see two gold rings, one in each of the man's nipples.

The man began playing with his nipples, alternating with pushing the boy's head down for cock duty.

The boy's mind reeled as he took it all in. He was sucking the cock of the Captain of this ship. With each passing moment, it got even better.

The Captain abruptly shoved Timothy away.

"Captain, Sir, what did I do wrong?"

"Nothing, son, lay on the bed, face down."

The boy complied nervously.

The Captain quickly removed his boots and then his clothing, abandoning them wherever he took them off. His Leather gloves remained in place. The Captain's body was flawless, a heavily muscled chest and his body a deepened tan. He marched over to the bed and quickly stripped the boy of his humble clothing. He lay on top of the boy and soon had maneuvered his hardened manhood into the boy's hole.

"This is known as buggering, son – most of the sailors on this ship do it to wile away the relentless hours. Some of them have wives back in the port, just like me, but being seamen, we rarely get to see our wives. The next best thing is a young man's handsome ass. Relax, Timothy, and enjoy the ride."

The Captain pounded his manflesh into the boy's ass. Timothy had never experienced such pain. He felt like his guts were being ripped asunder. Yet at the same time, it was pleasure beyond masturbation and the innocent adventures prompted by the wrestling he had enjoyed with his brothers.

The Captain gripped the back of the boy's hands as he continued to ride the young seaman's ass. The Captain's mantits pressed against the boy's back.

The Captain's sweat dripped down on the boy's back as he continued to pound his manflesh into the boy's ass. After a considerable length of time, Captain Breckenridge pumped a load of semen into the boy's hole.

The Captain lay panting for several minutes before rolling the boy over. He jammed his tongue down the boy's throat, gripping the boy's cheeks with his gloved hands. The Captain then proceeded to slap the boy's chest, pinch the boy's nipples, and manipulate the boy's cock and balls between the palms of his massive hands.

The boy forgot that he was with his Captain and responded. He reached up and kissed the Captain's lips, his cheeks, and his ringed nipples, until man and boy were engaged in fornicating like two wild animals. The boy grabbed the Captain's cock and balls and began manipulating them into a second frenzied hardness.

The Captain responded. He reached around and stuck first two fingers and then four fingers up the boy's ass, no longer virgin territory. The sensation of the man's fist up the boy's ass was without parallel in the young man's life.

Man and boy, Captain and seaman continued for some time until the Captain was sitting on the boy's chest, his arched cock poised inside the boy's mouth. He shot a second load of semen down the boy's willing throat. Simultaneously, the boy shot a load of his own which the Captain scooped up with his gloved hands and smeared on the boy's face and lips. The boy tasted the saltiness of the two juices combined – it was better than anything he had ever tasted. The scene was repeated virtually every night after that initial encounter. The Captain often called out his wife's name, Lucy, as he climaxed, but Tim didn't care. To him, the Captain was his worshipful Master and he was the Captain's suckslave.

The Captain and the boy experimented. The Captain delighted in trying new knots as restraints on the willing boy. At one point, Captain jammed a small whaletooth (the end was blunted) up his boy's willing ass. The tooth was carved with the suggestive phrase "Cap'n's Oar". The boy laid on the bed willingly as the man pierced the boy's tits with a heated needle. The Captain inserted gold rings.

The word aboard the ship soon made the rounds and the seamen were jealous of Tim. Carmichael, in particular, taunted Tim whenever he had the opportunity. Tim tried to ignore it. After all, he was just obeying the Captains orders. One night, however, Tim was attending to some duties which found him near Carmichael's station at starboard.

"Ya' think ya're pretty hot shit, being the Cap'n's woman, don't ya', O'Bryan?"

Tim ignored the taunting, but it continued.

"His last boy didn't pleasure him one night and he threw him overboard – eaten by the sharks... They bit off his cock just like ya' deserve, ya' little prick..."

Carmichael pushed the boy and the boy fell backward. Carmichael was on top of the boy, fumbling with the buttons on his pants. "I'll show ya' a real dick, boy."

As the boy struggled to regain his footing and push Carmichael off of him, Carmichael was lifted off of the boy by a pair of powerful, gloved hands belonging to Captain Breckenridge.

"Cap'n, Sir, we was only..."

The Captain backhanded Carmichael and dragged him below deck. Tim was ordered to follow.

The Captain quickly placed Carmichael in iron hand restraints. He pulled a bullwhip off a nearby nail.

The Captain administered ten lashes of the whip, each more painful than the last. Carmichael cried out in pain and his back was soon bloodied.

The Captain handed Tim the bullwhip and said, "Now, it's your turn, son."

Tim took the whip reluctantly, but with each of the ten blows, his whipping gained strength.

"Take that, you piece of shit," he yelled at Carmichael who was now crying in pain, "and don't let me see your face again."

Carmichael was unceremoniously thrown above board and he crawled to his sleeping quarters.

"Good work, son," the Captain said and the two retired to the Captain's quarters where they resumed their healthy session of mansex.

As the Captain unbuttoned his cod in anticipation of buggering his boy, a fierce storm blew up.

"Captain, captain, we're going down..." a panicked sailor cried as he pounded on the Captain's door.

Before the Captain could react, a swell of water broke down the door and the Captain and the boy were caught up in the swell. They were swept toward the door, which slammed shut, crushing the boy into the man's arms. Mercifully, the Captain and the boy drowned quickly.

In the year 2003, Peter Vandersloot and crew were conducting a deepwater archaeological recovery. The whaling ship, *The Pride of Nantucket* had been picked up on radar. It had gone down in 1853. Considering that the ship had been in its watery grave for over 150 years, it was remarkably intact. As the team investigated, two skeletons were found beneath deck.

An amused smile replaced the usual taciturn expression on Vandersloot's face because it surely looked as if the skeletons were engaged in a private moment. One male, about thirty, was lying on top of another male skeleton, about fifteen.

A total of four golden rings lay within the chest cavity of the boy. A fifth ring, still attached to a disintegrating Leather strap, lay fastened to the left leg.

HOT ASH, HOT ASS

Seemed like I was the only Leatherdaddy in the bar that night. I liked those odds.

I had arrived around nine and the crowd was kind of sparse. I ordered my beer and retreated to the patio where the bar owners still allowed men to smoke. And since I was a cigar smoker, it was crucial for me to frequent a bar where a man could still light up. I pulled out my cigar case and extracted a big fucker. As I pulled out the cigar clip from my pocket, a slender young man clad in chaps, tight blue jeans and a bar vest approached me.

"Please, Sir, allow me..."

I handed him the cigar and the clip and he clipped off the end. It dropped in his hand.

"Please, Sir, may I taste the clipped end?"

"Down on your knees, boy," I commanded and he dropped to his knees.

He bowed his head and presented his tongue for the receipt of the tip of the cigar.

"You didn't light my cigar, boy. Daddy's cigar comes before your pleasure…"

"I'm sorry, Sir, I wasn't thinking clearly." He reached in his back pocket and extracted a small pack of wooden matches. With that, I leaned down as he raised up and he lighted my cigar for me. I rotated it to get a full draw.

As I took my first exhale, I blew a smoke ring in his face. His eyes closed as he breathed in my smoke. He presented me with the tip and I motioned for him to open his mouth. He thanked me as I dropped the tip in his mouth. He kneeled silently as I continued to draw. He was cute, but a little on the slim side, so I dismissed him, telling him to come back later. He withdrew.

I propped my booted foot against the wall and watched the ebb and flow of men in and out of the patio door.

One guy definitely caught my eye. He was heavily muscled, with big pecs stretching the 'USMC' tee shirt he wore. Leather cods and predictably, military boots with his pants tucked neatly into the tops of the spit-shined boots. As he sauntered to the bar, I took in the bulge in his cod and the tightness of the Leathers against his ass cheeks. His muscular ass hardened my cock. Now, that's a boy that I could be interested in. I hastily prepared a mental list of where I wanted to place my cock.

He retrieved his beer and cruised the area. He wore blue mirrored glasses like me. Short-cropped crewcut. Solid features, clean-shaven. As he checked me out, I felt his eyes linger on me. I was in full black Leather, with my studded cod in place. Damascus gloves, spit-shined Dehners, Muir cap.

We were playing the cat and mouse game and I looked indifferently away. However, I took a long draw on my cigar and then began absently massaging my cod with cigar in hand. It did not escape his attention as I caught him looking at me again when I looked over in his direction. He averted his eyes only after a long pause.

"Come to Daddy," I attempted to telepathically tell him, "Boys come to Daddies."

He remained where he was but I could see the gears clicking.

He absently rubbed his muscled chest and took several more swigs of beer. He gripped the bottle with an iron grip. Damn! I wanted this boy in my dungeon. The ash on my cigar was lengthening as we continued to play this game.

An older guy, heavily tattooed and in biker gear, approached me and we started chatting. "Sir, I'm a cigar pig, and... and I couldn't help but notice that your cigar will soon need servicing...," he said.

All the time, my eyes drifted over to the muscle boy – he remained where he had been standing, glancing away but I could still feel his eyes watching me.

"Yes, son, it will soon need to find an ashtray."

The tattooed biker dropped to his knees in front of me and opened his mouth. He placed his arms behind his back, revealing two pierced nips.

I flicked the ash onto his tongue and he thanked me as he thoughtfully ingested the ash.

"Good boy" as I motioned for him to rise. I placed the lighted cigar against his right nip and then his left nip, heating up the rings. I massaged his tits with my gloved hands in between 'heatings'. As I continued to work the tattooed boy's tits, I glanced over to find the muscle boy. He had momentarily turned away, his tight, handsome ass beckoning me to break my own rules.

Momentarily distracted, I refocused my attentions on the biker boy when he said, "Thank you, Sir." I thanked him for his services and sent him on his way. I wanted that muscle boy's ass and cock in my dungeon.

Horny as hell, I was once alone. But the muscle boy had turned around and I caught him eyeing me once again. I began a more vigorous massage of my cod with the hand that held the lighted cigar. I leaned my head back, lost in my own reverie of self-stimulation. Thinking of that thick cock and that beautiful ass. I knew that I had captured his attention. I knew it was only a matter of time. A large boy, clad in a motorcycle jacket, approached me, but I dismissed him, telling him "I'm waiting for someone..." Well, it was the truth – I had set my sights on the muscle boy.

After seeing me with this boy (actually the third of the evening), I guess the muscle boy thought he had better take action because he rushed over.

"Sir, I'm Tony. I have to tell you that I really enjoyed seeing you in action with your cigar sub."

I thanked him and introduced myself.

"Is he the only boy that services your cigar, Sir?"

I revealed to him that I had never seen the boy before.

Tony seemed relieved when he said, "I will bet you get a lot of offers, Sir."

"Can't complain," I offered him a puff of my cigar. He inhaled deeply.

As he was inhaling, I casually reached down and squeezed his cod. It was packed with what I knew was a thick, veined cock and meaty balls. My cock started hardening.

"Sir, thank you, Sir, I... uh, would like to take your ash, Sir, if that's... uh, permissible."

I assured him it was as I placed my arm around his shoulder and drew him closer to me. "Mine, all mine," I seemed to say as my hand squeezed his shoulder, "Keep away from my boy and me." We chatted while the ash lengthened on my cigar. He revealed that he was just recently out of the Marine Corps – seven years of duty which included a two-year stint of hard-fighting in Iraq. "I've had this interest in Leather for a long time, Sir."

I assured him that I was a pure-bred Leatherman – committed to my proud lifestyle, defiant to all who would criticize it.

"You look so handsome in it, Sir."

The ash lengthened and looked as if it was about to drop. I ordered this beefy ex-Marine down on his knees in front of me. He dropped as if taking orders from a drill sergeant.

I ordered for him to open his mouth, warning him of the slight burn he would feel.

He took my ash willingly.

"Fuck...," he moaned, "That tastes so good."

"Well, son, I have something else that would taste equally good" as I pressed his mouth into my packed cod.

Aware that this was a public place, however, I abruptly stopped the scene before he went any further. We finished our beers and I escorted him back to my dungeon.

As his temporary Drill Sergeant, I ordered him to strip which he did without question. He was a fucking knock out, with muscled arms, chest, legs, and as predicted, a heavily-veined cock and two low hangers.

I manacled him to my work-over table with heavy Leather straps.

Even though it seemed a crime, I hooded him with my bondage hood. He accepted it without question.

"Thank you, Sir," as I blew smoke in his face.

My cigar from the bar was almost three-quarters gone and so, I told him that I would like another cigar.

"I like them warmed up, son." He didn't understand the implication of this. I pulled an empty cigar tube from my stockpile of toys. I inserted one of my stogies in it and, leaning over him, "I want you to keep it warm for me, son."

His eyes still registered puzzlement. I lifted his ass off the table and slowly inserted the tube up his boyhole.

He moaned as it was being inserted but said, "Thank you, Sir, I'll keep it warm for you."

As he lay there, vulnerable and naked, I couldn't resist. I climbed on top of him and felt his masculine body underneath my own masculine, Leathered body.

His cock quickly responded to my studded cod. I felt it harden underneath my own swollen cock. I reached my Leather gloved hands underneath his muscular shoulders. My tongue met his tongue through the Leather hood. We kissed long and hard.

Leather against skin. My tits ached from the nipclamps on my tits as they pressed into his beefy pecs.

Our cocks swollen, with only a Leather cod separating them.

I don't know how long we remained frozen in this position, our bodies gyrating, a combination of my Leather masculinity and his nakedness.

He attempted to speak. I released his tongue from my mouth.

"Sir, I have to shoot..." he begged.

My swollen cock was ready as well. I reached down and unsnapped my cod. Our hardened rods finally met side by side and within a short period of time, we both shot simultaneously. We both screamed "FUCK!" as our cumjuices combined and slathered our bodies and my Leather in a fuckfest of semen.

"Fuck!" the boy moaned as I continued to rub our man and boy cum all over his naked body. We kissed again, long and hard.

My cock was dripping and so was his. I climbed off of him and released him from his manacles. I ordered him on his knees where he was commanded to lick the cum off my dick.

It felt so fucking good that I achieved a second erection. His tongue flicked in and out of my piss slit until I could not control a second load of cum which shot down his throat. He began cleaning my Leathers.

"Son, my cigar went out. I'm ready for my second cigar." With that, he dropped to all fours and presented his ass to me. He had kept the cigar tube safe and warm in his hole.

"Your's to take, Sir. When you are ready, Sir," he responded. I assumed he meant both cigar and ass, and I intended to have both.

I extracted the cigar. He clipped and lighted it, and presented it to me, with his head bowed. I ordered him to lean against the workover table. I stood with my legs squarely apart and spread his asscheeks. That handsome ass was crying out for an exploration of my manrod. Just too tempting.

I lubed my dick with the cum which still remained on the legs of my pants. My cock slid easily up his hole. He gripped the edge of the table as it inched up his rectum. When I was fully inside, I wrapped my arms around his torso and began pulling on his handsome tits. My rockhard cock slid in and out of that handsome ass as if I was drilling for oil.

When I had worked on his tits for some time, I began playing with his cock which had not softened. It was a beautiful cock. The Leather of my Damascus gloves had the desired effect and soon, the boy asked permission to shoot. I denied him permission and he winced as he attempted to keep his cum under control. After all, my cock was still deeply imbedded in his military terrain.

"Sir, please Sir," he begged as his cock throbbed up and down. As I had already cum twice, I rationalized that the boy deserved some consideration. I withdrew my cock. I surprised him when I turned him around and squatted down, taking his cock in my mouth. As a top, I don't often swallow a boy's cum, but this boy's handsome cock was just too appealing. I swallowed his dick and he soon came down my throat.

Our session lasted a little longer but we eventually retired to the shower where we continued to play. Naked man flesh against the flesh of this fucking handsome boy. I pulled him close to me until our cocks were side-by-side, both pointing north. Although we didn't shoot this time, our cocks were erect the whole time. We toweled each other off and retired to my back porch, both naked. I dropped into a chair and indicated he should do the same. I rewarded him with a cigar and I selected one for myself. However, it wasn't long before the boy said, "Sir? May I approach you?

I gave him permission and he dropped to his knees, ready to service my cock once again. It was obvious that the Marines had trained this boy well.

A Boner Book

SEDUCTION OF
A LEATHERBOY

Steve and I had met at the Cellblock in Chicago after a year of raunchy and passionate talk over the internet on a Leather website. Our bond was instant, we were Leatherbrothers under our black skins. Our conversations were fiery and dirty, filled with claims of each being the bigger Leatherman.

After meeting, we rendezvoused in Pennsylvania and had a S&M filled weekend, only fueling our lust for one another. We fucked the whole time he was here and when he left, I knew I would soon follow suit, to have more of the same in his native Michigan. It seemed an eternity before I could clear my desk at work for a week's vacation. I eventually did, fueled by my horniness, and soon had my Leather gear and my bag of toys packed. I rushed to Steve's secluded estate in Michigan.

Within a few minutes of my arrival, we were tearing at each other like the horny Leathermen we were. I'm no going to recount those adventures at this point, however, I may tell about them at some future time. Suffice it to say, we had a great couple of days.

Steve is an excellent cook and fed me like royalty. On the third night after a great dinner, we were sitting in front of his fireplace, with drinks and cigars.

"I want you to take me to the bar you were talking about...," I began.

"It's a man's bar, you might not fit in..." he taunted.

"Bitch, they let you in, don't they?"

We threw bullshit at each other all the time.

The next evening, we were both dressed in our heaviest Leather jackets with chrome, our spiked cods, Wescos, Muir caps, et al. We were dressed to kill, or more appropriately, seduce. We had decided to add a boy to the mix – one we could both work over to our mutual satisfaction.

We mounted his Harley and were soon cruising to Detroit.

Like many Leather bars, it was in a sleazy part of town – but I felt sleazy. My cod was packed with my over-anxious cock. We parked the cycle and marched down the street. Several guys cruised us, but by a mutual nod, they weren't appropriate. For one thing, no Leather, just jeans and tee shirts.

We marched into the bar, drawing the attention of a number of bar patrons. Steve headed to the back of the bar, which was darker. Groping and fondling was tolerated as long as it didn't get out of hand. We both placed our beer orders and then established our turf along the darkened wall.

Boys, and a few Leathermen, began to make their appearance. But they seemed intimidated to even say 'Hello' to us. The first hour or so was pretty pathetic and I was beginning to regret my decision. We could be playing.

By and by, a friend of Steve's, a healthy-looking Leatherman, showed up and we chatted with him for a while. My eyes were on cruise control, of course. "Pretty slim pickings," I was thinking as a handsome young lad caught my eye. It was obvious that he was new to the Leather bar scene. He apparently was alone, as he strolled through the bar, not making eye contact with anyone.

He wore a cycle jacket, but it was brand new. It had the sheen of newness as did his wispy brown hair – did he get a haircut to come to the bar? Although his hair still fell over his right eye, adding that look of boyish innocence. He sported a rim beard and a bushy mustache. He wore a pristine white tee shirt (also new) and a tight necklace of puka beads (or at least that's what they were called in the 1970s). He was slender, carrying my eyes right down to his tight little blue jeans and a pair of Wescos up to his knee. Not scuffed, brand new. I could see the faint outline of his cock, arched in the crotch of his pants. Now, he might be a little too slender for Steve, but I knew that I wanted to see that boy stretched out on a bondage table, a smoke-hood covering that tousled hair, and my gloved hands exploring that handsome little ass. Laying my cat-o-nine tails repeatedly across his back and ass.

The boy looked nervously around, holding his beer by the neck of the bottle. Taking nervous little swigs. Jamming one hand in his pocket. Trying to look tough, I guess.

My cock hardened in my cod and was now jutting forward like a dowsing rod seeking water.

Steve continued his conversation with his friend, so, I began absently fondling my crotch. I cocked my head to the left and began staring at that cute little number.

He glanced over at me, but quickly averted his eyes when I tried to make eye contact.

He moved to the side wall and looked absently across the bar room. But, I caught him locking out of the corner of his eye at me.

I continued for a few more seconds to rub my crotch and then slowly moved toward him.

Even though he pretended not to notice, I could see his eyes shift back and forth frequently, noting my progress.

Eventually, I stood beside him. He pretended to study a group of guys who had just entered the bar.

He took several more nervous swigs of his bottle which was my cue.

"Let me buy you another beer... is that your brand of choice?"

"Uh, yeah, but that's not necessary..." he said nervously.

"It will be my pleasure, son." With that I hastened to the bar. Out of the corner of my eye I could see that he stood frozen in place. I just hoped no one else would swoop in on my chosen territory. For once, I was lucky. He remained standing in place.

I handed him the fresh beer and I held the bottle up to click it against his. "Here's to new friendships, son. What's your name?"

"Uh, Brian..."

"You new to the Leather scene, son?"

"Uh, no, no, I've been coming here for years."

"Really, son? I'm glad to know that. I think the bartender is a pretty hot guy, the guy over there with the harness on. What's his name – I can't remember? I wouldn't mind hooking up with him... You know him?"

"Uh, no, I don't know him... he must be new."

"Oh," I feigned disappointment. We took several more swigs of our beers and I puffed on my cigar for a few more minutes.

"Is there a play area here, son? My testosterone level is high tonight."

The boy confessed that he didn't know if the bar had a play area, but "they remodeled it last year and I, uh, haven't been here much since the remodeling..."

"Dig it deeper, boy," I thought to myself, "I'll catch you yet."

"Oh, I just thought a hot stud like you would be here every week..."

"Uh, no, no, I've been busy..."

"Oh, really. Yeah, work sure as hell interferes with your social life, doesn't it? Looks like you just got paid – bought some new Leather for yourself. Where'd you get your jacket?"

He told me and I pretended to recognize the name of the local Leathergoods dealer. I asked him to turn around so I could see the back.

"Looks damned fine, son. Looks very handsome. Oh, your epaulet is unsnapped, son, let me fix it for you..." With that I reached up and pretended to resnap his epaulet. I left my hand casually on his shoulder. He made no motions to pull away.

"Tell me something, son. Is this your first time in a Leather bar?" I looked straight into his green eyes.

"No," he started, but then he looked away quickly, and finally said, "Yes, it is. Is it obvious?"

"Yeah, son. Your Leathers look brand new. Once you get to a few Leather bars and play a little, they'll look just like what other Leatherguys have on."

For the first time during our conversation, he seemed to relax.

"I was afraid to come to the bar in just jeans and a tee shirt..."

"I'll tell you something, son. Honestly, you look good in your gear. Just needs to be broken in a little" And if that boy only knew that I had in mind to break in not only his Leathers, but his handsome body as well!

"I do?"

"Yes, son, you look very handsome." With that I reached my hand down to pat him on the ass.

"Thank you. Thank you." He seemed to relax even more, as if taking a deep sigh. He moved a little closer to me.

"Can I tell you something?"

"What's that, son?"

"You are so handsome. You look so awesome in your Leather outfit."

"Well, thank you, son. There was a time when I was the new Leatherguy in the bar." I recounted an incident in my early barlife. I patted him on the ass again and then drew him toward me with my right hand. My other hand pulled his ass even closer to me. I could see that his cock had hardened in his blue jeans.

"You are the kind of man I've had wet dreams about," he said.

With that, I pulled him even closer and stroked his beard. I smiled at him. I pulled his mouth toward mine and we engaged in a long kiss. His arms tentatively moved to embrace me. I guided them around me and then held him closely.

"Well, I see you have made a new friend..." It was Steve's slightly sarcastic voice that I heard over my shoulder.

We separated.

"Steve, this handsome young man is Brian. Brian, this is my friend Steve."

"Oh, uh, how do you do?" Brian said nervously.

"Don't let him bother you, Brian, we have an open relationship. He's only my partner for the week," I said, trying to sound reassuringly.

Within a few minutes, Steve had warmed up to my boy of choice and apparently approved of my captured prey.

Steve could be charming and soon had the boy relaxed, just as I had done.

Steve went to retrieve a round of beers and while he was getting them, Brian said, "I don't want to interfere with you guys – I'd better be going..."

"No, son, I don't want you to go anywhere except back in your rightful place, protected by your Daddy's arms."

I encircled his cute body with my arms and we were soon engaged in a kissing session, fondling Leather and denim.

It was apparent that the boy had fallen for me and would now do anything I ordered him to.

I casually brought up my interest in S&M.

"I've always been curious, but have not tried any... of it," he said hesitantly.

"Well, son, let this Daddy guide you."

"Oh, oh, I don't know..."

"Can a Leatherman who kisses you so passionately be all that bad?" as I raised his chin so our tongues touched.

We once again kissed long and hard.

Steve came back with a fresh round of beers. We all took several long swallows of beer as Steve and I puffed on our cigars.

"Steve, I think this young man would like to see your house. Brian, it's over one hundred fifty years old, hand-hewn beams, a huge fireplace... come on with us and spend the night."

He hesitated.

"Daddy's orders, son," I commanded and I hugged his shoulders protectively. The boy shook his head 'Yes'.

We exited the bar and I hopped in the boy's car. Mounting his cycle, Steve led us back to his den of iniquity.

The boy stood uncertainly in the hallway until I guided him to the Leather sofa. I sat on one side, Steve settled in on the other side.

I fondled his crotch while Steve rubbed his shoulders.

"Loosen up, son. You're among men who admire handsome young men." The boy seemed more nervous.

I reached up and unbuckled his jacket belt and then unbuttoned the top of his jeans.

Both the Leathermen's cods were bulging. The boy's cock had risen nicely in his tight jeans.

I continued to rub his denimed crotch, holding my other hand protectively around his shoulder. Steve rose from the couch to get us drinks. So what if the boy's drink was laced with a little more alcohol than ours.

I fondled the boy's already tousled hair and pulled him toward my Leather-covered chest. He began to respond by tentatively rubbing my chest.

I kissed him on the forehead. "That feels nice, son. But your hand would certainly be welcome down here" as I guided his hand to my hardened crotch.

The boy responded. He was rubbing my cod when Steve brought us our drinks and supplied me and himself with a cigar.

I tentatively blew a puff of smoke in the boy's face. He seemed to follow the smoke to the point of origin. "Daddy," he said, "that smells so good. Do it again, please."

I obliged, all the while continuing to excite his cock and reaching with my other hand, slowly pulling on his nips through the tee shirt.

"Why don't we get that jacket and shirt of you, so we can see your handsome chest?" He slowly removed the articles of clothing and revealed a handsome, boyish chest.

"That's much better, son. You are handsome." Steve echoed my sentiment.

With a few swigs of alcohol and some coaxing from his newly-found Daddies, we soon had the boy naked. Trim and athletic. He was handsome – I had made a good choice.

We began a more aggressive exploration. The boy didn't seem to mind as we continued our cock-hardening activity.

When I thought he was ready, I asked him to kneel in front of me. I unsnapped my cod and my hard cock sprang forth. I didn't even have to ask as the boy began a moist tonguing of the cockhead and the shaft.

Even though he was new to the Leather scene, he certainly made up for lost time.

His head was bobbing up and down on my cock until I shot a load down his throat.

After he licked it dry, Steve pulled him gently over to him and he performed the same service for Steve.

After he had serviced both of us, he looked inquisitively up at me. I reached down and pulled on the boy's cock and within a few seconds, he shot a load of cum onto the floor.

His head arched back as he continued to rub his cock.

"Thank you, Daddies, that felt awesome... I've never shot a load that felt so good."

"We'll continue to guide you, son, to even more pleasurable experiences. Are you a willing boy?"

"Oh, yes, Daddy."

We guided the boy downstairs to Steve's dungeon. The boy did not flinch this time when he saw the St. Andrew's cross or the bondage table.

Maybe he didn't quite know what was about to transpire.

I slowly added the wrist restraints and ankle restraints and secured him to the St. Andrew's cross.

Steve and I alternated as we flogged the boy's virgin ass and back. Both of us had re-established hard cocks in our Leather cods.

The boy took it well. I asked him several times if he was okay. He assured me he was. I introduced the smoke hood to him before placing it over his head. I placed the blindfold in place as well as the mouth plug.

Steve and I played with one another for a few minutes while the boy became accustomed to his hood.

We continued the flogging and introduced several new paddles and whips to the rotations. The boy's flesh was fresh with red marks.

I began rubbing that cute little ass for the next assault. I greased up my right glove and slowly inserted my fingers into his tight hole. He flinched, but as I massaged it, he once again became relaxed and even arched his ass upward, ready to receive my gloved hand.

Steve fondled the boy's dick which was once again hardened.

"You are a good boy. Do you think you can take Daddy's cock up your ass?," I asked. The boy's head nodded 'Yes".

With some lube, I eased my cock up his ass. It was as if the boy had been born to be the receptacle for my cock. After I had planted my seed, Steve did the same.

We took the boy off the St. Andrew's cross only to reposition him with his back to it.

I have a devious little cat-o-nine tails with metal tips. Time to see if the boy could take a cock-flogging. And he did, the boy did beautifully. With each new plateau we introduced him to, he seemed to respond even more enthusiastically. Sometimes, a submissive boy can be so eager to learn that they will take whatever you give them without question.

We felt that the boy had done well and so, we both fondled, squeezed and pulled on his cock and balls until he shot a massive load on our Leather gloves. Now ordinarily, a boy would be punished for this infraction, but not this night. The boy had done well and we wanted him to enjoy his entry into Leatherboyhood.

We escorted him back upstairs and offered him a cigar. He gratefully took it. He knelt between us, alternately laying his head on my knee and then Steve's. We continued to massage his body with our gloved hands.

"Thank you, Daddies, this was so special for me..." and he started crying.

I pulled him toward me, kissed him lightly, and we escorted him to our bedroom, where he lay in the comfort of our bed. Nestled between his two Leatherdaddies like the affectionate pup he was.

Twice, we woke him from his sleep. In turn, we each mounted him and plunged our cocks into his hole.

When he fell asleep after the second assault, Steve and I retired to the playroom to play a little more – after all, we were used to marathon fucking. The boy made both of us horny as hell.

When we returned to the bedroom, the boy was sleeping peacefully. Although it was hard to resist, we let him sleep. He had earned it. Tomorrow we would continue his education.

THE RED BANDANA

I watched him for three weeks, hidden in a grove of trees.

I waited for him to return home in his business suit and tie. As regular as clockwork, he entered his house, only to emerge ten minutes later in his black Leather skins. Leather pants with an attached, studded codpiece. Wristbands with studs. Military boots, spit-shined and tightly-laced, his pant legs neatly folded into the tops. Never wore a shirt. His beautiful mantits flexed as he moved. Sometimes he wore a pair of skintight black Leather gloves, other times he wore tan Leather workgloves to work on his landscaping. A cigar was usually clenched between his teeth.

As my lusting eyes followed his every move while he was outside, I knew that routine too. He would inspect his property starting from the left and making a wide circle. He looked at every bush and every plant, occasionally pulling off a leaf or a dead flowerhead. As he inspected, he would often reach down to fondle his codpiece or rub his muscular arms or pecs. I licked my lips because I wanted to be that hand rubbing those areas, my mouth sucking on his nipples or on that loaded cod.

Two thirds of the way of the inspection, he always came perilously close to the grove of trees. I stood frozen, afraid to move or even to breathe. He seemed lost in his own reverie of communing with nature, however, unaware that a boy lusted after him. I longed to step forward and make my presence known, to beg him to take me as his boy. Still, I felt unworthy of this beautiful specimen of manflesh.

When he returned to his house, I usually crept up to the property and retraced his footsteps. If I was lucky, I would find the dropped ash from his cigar. I would flop down on the ground and tongue the collected ash into my mouth. I would savor the taste of it until it dissolved, leaving a slightly salty taste in my mouth. It connected me to him and I relished that feeling, ever so slight. You have to understand that my Father had deserted us when I was a kid and I had never been intimate with anyone except my cousin Jess when we were fourteen and fifteen respectively. This man was handsome and strong and was in control of the world around him. I wanted to be with him, be an intimate part of his life.

One day, as I watched, the Leatherman pulled his beautiful cock out of the cod and after massaging it for some time, he leaned against a tree and jacked off. A load of cum shot forward. I gulped as I knew I had to taste the Leathercum in my mouth. He had barely closed the back door of his house when I leapt forward and pouncing on the wet grass, I licked every drop I could find. As I licked it up, my dick became aroused and I retreated to the grove of trees, leaned against a tree, and jacked off just as the Leatherman had.

The very next day, the Leatherdaddy did the same inspection and stopping in virtually the same place, the Leatherman pulled off his cod and once again began to massage his dick. This time, however, he released a stream of piss near the base of the tree. My cock was already hard by the time I reached the tree and I licked the wet bark of the tree and the glistening grass underneath it. It was like tasting the finest wine. I knew the tap from which it came.

An unbelievably lucky third day followed. The Leatherman came out for his usual inspection, and my eyes followed his every move. As he stopped at his jack-off tree, I stopped breathing. *"Master, I will take either your cum or your piss,"* I begged silently, *"but please, please leave something for your boy..."* He unsnapped the codpiece and withdrew his handsome mancock. It was beautiful and I only wished I had the courage to run forward, fall on my knees, and suck on his knob. The Daddy pulled out a red bandana from his left rear pocket. He rubbed the bandana against the shaft of the cock as the cock became more and more aroused. The cock pulsated, arching toward the sky.

The Daddy squeezed the shaft of his cock with his gloved hand, enveloping his hard manrod with the red bandana. His back arched against the tree as this boy looked on. I couldn't breathe, my dick was hardened in my jeans, and my hand was furiously rubbing my dickhead through the softened denim fabric.

The Leatherman continued to stroke his meat. It was torturous. His meat got thicker and bigger as mine exploded in my pants. The Daddy continued the rhythm of stroking his dickshaft with the red bandana. He began moaning softly and his legs seemed to buckle as he shot what I assume was a huge load in the bandana.

He stood panting for several minutes as I convinced myself that he would not be happy if I made my presence known at this point. It took a lot of convincing not to run out there, drop to my knees, and beg to lick the cum off his dickhead.

The Leatherman, now recovered, absently tucked the red bandana in his back pocket and headed for the back door.

I rushed forward, hoping that the bandana had not caught every drop of this man's cum. I needed to taste his cum. I needed to swallow it and savor it. I needed to rub it on my own cock.

Despite my search, I could not find one drop of residue. I was practically frantic when I noticed a patch of red lying near the back door of the Leatherman's house. It was the cum-soaked red bandana! I had to retrieve it – it contained that handsome man's jism. I crept silently forward and reaching the bandana, I pounced on it like some wild animal. I opened the bandana to find the recently-shot load. I started licking the soaked cloth, tasting the saltiness of that handsome Leatherman's cum.

"If you like it that much, boy, why didn't you come directly to the source?" said a voice on the porch. As I looked up from my position on the ground with the cum-soaked rag in my mouth, I couldn't speak. The Leatherman was advancing toward me until he was standing directly over me, his booted feet spread on either side of my shoulders. His codpiece was directly above my head. I still was speechless. He unsnapped his cod, pulled out his dick, and proceeded to direct a stream of his hot man piss in my face. I have never tasted anything better as I attempted to catch every delicious drop.

"Oh, Sir, please...," I started, but I fell silent, embarrassed, not knowing what to say.

"On your feet, boy."

I slowly rose to my feet. The Daddy grabbed me roughly by the back of the neck and escorted me down a short flight of steps into his dark basement.

As my naive eyes adjusted, I made out a seven foot table with straps and rings on it. It was covered in black Leather.

"Lie face down on the table, boy."

When I hesitated, I was unceremoniously thrown on the table. The Leatherman secured my wrists and ankles in place with the broad Leather straps. My head was positioned so that I could observe the Leatherman's actions. I began to heave nervously and tears welled up in my eyes.

"Relax, son, you've been watching me for some time, now it's my turn." So, he knew I had been stalking him.

"Just so you won't make too much noise, here's a souvenir." With that, the Leatherman stuffed the red bandana in my mouth.

Despite my fear, tasting the man's cum on the bandana was a stimulant and I could feel my dick harden against the table.

Momentarily distracted, I looked back at the Leatherman. He had slipped on a black Leather hood. His piercing blue eyes stared at me, emotionless. His right hand held a small black

Leather whip. His hands were encased in the tight black Leather gloves.

The lashing began on my back and ass. It felt relaxing, no more than a gentle tap. Then the Leatherman increased the lashing in speed and in intensity. I squeezed my eyes shut as the strips of Leather connected with my shoulder blades, my rib cage, and my asscheeks.

I wanted to plead with him for it to stop but I couldn't utter a sound with the bandana in place.

After what seemed an eternity, the lashings did stop.

The Leatherman leaned down, grabbed my jaw so that we made eye contact and said, *"That was Session One, boy. Are you ready for Session Two?"*

Tears welled up in my eyes, but I all I could do was weakly shake my head, *"Yes."*

The Leatherman repositioned me, lying on my back. The black Leather covering felt good on my reddened ass and back.

My newly-found Leatherdaddy placed a black Leather bag around my cock and balls. It was snapped tightly into place and a padlock was added. Not only was I a prisoner, so were my privates.

The Daddy then pulled a hook down from the ceiling and attached the padlock to the hook. He pulled the chain upward, increasing the pressure on my cock and balls. He then pulled a second hook down from the ceiling and attached that to a pair of nipple clamps. The nipple clamps were soon biting into the virgin flesh of my nipples. The pain was excruciating. I wrenched my head from side to side and cried as best I could for him to stop. When my body lurched, the pain on my cock and balls made me cry even more.

"You'll get used to the pain, boy." the Leatherman attempted to reassure me.

He began lashing me with the same Leather whip. After a while, I didn't notice the pain in my nipples because I was now concentrating on the repeated assault on my chest.

"When will this end?" I thought.

The Daddy stopped after what seemed a second eternity. I was so grateful – I began to cry.

The Leatherman didn't seem to notice as he pulled a cigar case from his back pants' pocket. He lighted a big cigar, standing back and watching me. The ash lengthened on his cigar. He approached the table and pulling the bandana out of my mouth, he gruffly said, *"This should bring back some memories"* as he flicked the hot ash onto my tongue.

It burned, but oddly enough, it brought back the pleasant memory of me licking up his discarded ash in the yard not so long ago.

It was at that point, that I realized that my fantasy had come true. I was in the presence of this handsome Leatherman and he was giving me my fantasy. It was a turning point and I began to relax and really enjoy my time with the Leatherman. He was in charge and I knew he would guide me wisely in this new journey. I was his boy, he was my Daddy.

The abuse continued but I enjoyed it with a renewed willingness. I submitted to the Leatherdaddy's sessions which continued long into the evening and each day as the Leatherman returned from work.

Now when my Daddy comes home, I no longer hide. I am there as his willing and eager boy, waiting on the steps, a red bandana positioned in my mouth. *"Take me to the basement, Sir."* I humbly say. I've asked him lots of questions and he has always answered them patiently. One mysterious answer though was received when I asked why there was always a red bandana in his left rear pocket. He smiled, and said, *"That's Lesson #20 and I'll explore that in de-tail."* Hmmm, wonder what that meant?

THE BARN

Dane woke early on Saturday morning and his first thoughts were of putting on his buttery soft Leathers. They were expensive Italian Leathers and fit his slender body like a glove. Tight pants, jacket with racing stripe down the shoulders, skin-tight black gloves, Tony Lama cowboy boots, and his helmet. He gulped a cup of coffee and set off on his equally expensive BMW motorcycle.

He exited the expressway as soon as he could and was soon zipping along country roads in rural Bucks County. Dane was a student of architecture at the University of Pennsylvania and was working on his Master's thesis, analyzing the stone barns which dotted the landscape. He had one in mind that he wanted to explore that morning and had put his camera and other equipment in his saddlebags. This particular barn, most probably on private property, was one which he had only viewed from a distance and that was his goal to explore. Dane was a smooth talker and he knew that if he could find the owner he would be able to explore the barn with freedom.

He circled the area at least three times before he saw the barn in a distance. The barn was isolated but there was an old frame farmhouse a distance away from it. Still, he couldn't immediately find any access to either location. He retraced his ride. He stopped and started several times before he finally saw a dirt lane. An unfriendly sign proclaimed that there was to be 'No Trespassing' on the property. Dane blithely ignored the sign, confident that he was above the warning. He opened the gate and zoomed down the dirt lane. It wound on for approximately half a mile until finally emerging into the clearing with the farmhouse. The grounds were in good repair, although there was no immediate sign of life.

A nearby shed, however, revealed a magnificent gleaming Harley Low Rider. Dane instinctively knew that he now had an immediate camaraderie with the owner – he knew his cycles. He politely knocked on the door of the farmhouse. There was no answer even after repeated knocking. He stood for a good ten minutes before deciding that he would march toward the barn. He left his cycle in the yard and trooped across the fields toward the barn.

He turned back toward the house, but no one had appeared. The surroundings were eerily quiet and Dane wondered briefly if he should turn back.

The barn was a good solid barn of late 18th century construction and had meticulous restoration to the stonework. He photographed the approach to the barn from various angles. Still, eerily quiet. His ears strained to hear any sounds. Occasionally, he thought he heard the rattling of metal chains.

Dane shot several rolls of film before approaching the wide barn door. It appeared to be early nineteenth century. Painted milk paint red. Strap hinges. Rosehead nails.

He approached the door and a slight shuffling and rattling of chains greeted his now-alert ears.

"Hello, hello..." Dane yelled, cupping his hands around his mouth.

A brief groan greeted him.

"Whaa..." Dane started to say, as he entered the barn.

Horse stalls, he noted in his mind, were probably late 19th-early 20th century. He stepped into the darkness of the barn. The groan seemed to come from the back of the barn and Dane marched toward the back.

His jaw dropped as he viewed two young, naked men chained to the back wall of the barn.

Despite his trepidation at continuing, he strode confidently to the two, handsome young men. Dane had visited the Leather bars in Philadelphia and had toyed with the idea of bondage but had never witnessed it in real life. This was real life, and despite his own confidence, he was ready to turn tail and run.

He approached the boys, both of whom had gags in their mouths. Dane thought the fellows looked familiar and it dawned on him that they were fellow students at the University of Pennsylvania. He hastily removed the gags and questioned, "Who did this to you?"

The boys, both groggy and covered in lash marks, only shook their heads.

One finally responded, "Get out, while you have a chance... he'll be back soon..."

"Who?"

"Me, asshole" a gruff voice answered and before Dane could respond, a muscular Leatherman emerged from the shadows and quickly handcuffed Dane's hands behind his back.

Dane gave quite a struggle, but it was to no avail. The man was bigger and brawnier than Dane.

Dane was quickly shackled next to the other boys along the wall.

He kicked the Leatherman and received a slap across the face.

His feet were soon in leg irons.

Dane couldn't help but look at his captor. He viewed a muscular Leatherman, dressed in a motorcycle hat, a heavy Leather motorcycle jacket with chains attached to the left epaulet, a heavy Leather harness, studded, fingerless gloves, black

Leather pants with a studded codpiece, and Wesco boots laced to the knees. Despite his fears, he felt sure that he could talk his way out of the situation, after all they both belonged to the brotherhood of cyclemen and they were both men of the black skins. Maybe he could help the other captured boys, too.

"Please, Sir, I really meant no harm, I was just photographing your barn..."

"Shut the fuck up..." as the Leatherman stuffed a gag in Dane's mouth. Dane tried valiantly to spit it out.

The Leatherman just laughed and pulled a whip off his belt.

"Let me look at you," said the Leatherman, as he zipped open Dane's jacket and pants.

The man roughly squeezed Dane's cock and balls as he pulled them out.

"Well, you're a pretty boy, aren't you? Nice Leathers, son. You won't be needing them for a while." With that he pulled the boy's pants down around his boots.

The Leatherman whipped the boy's cock and balls, and despite the boy's fear, his cock was soon arching upward.

Dane cranked up his courage and with one mighty spit, spit out the gag and managed to spit on the Leatherman.

For that, he was lashed across the chest with the whip and slapped across the face repeatedly with the Leatherman's big, meaty hands. It brought tears to the boy's eyes.

"Boys pay for disrespecting their Leatherdaddy."

The whippings and slappings continued for several hours before the Leatherman backed off abruptly. He exited the barn.

Dane was in pain, but felt oddly stimulated by the whippings and bondage. His arms ached from being suspended above his head and his legs were falling asleep. His Leathers were becoming uncomfortable as the barn heated up with the sun arching across the sky.

Sometime later, the barn door opened and all three boys looked expectantly at the Leatherman. He carried a squeeze bottle of water to each boy and they all gulped thirstily as if they had never tasted anything better.

Dane once again tried to reason with the Leatherman. "Please, Sir," he said, "I meant no disrespect. I am a student of architecture at the University of Pennsylvania. I am studying stone barn construction..." his voice trailed off, because the Leatherman didn't appear to be paying one God's bit of attention to him.

The Leatherman appeared to be preoccupied with lighting a cigar, but answered, "That does not entitle you to trespass on another's property. I have chased off more than a few students of art and architecture, historic preservation methods, and on, and on. It's private property, boy. Turn about is fair play – you violated my property, now, I'm violating your's – mainly you."

He sidled over to Dane and blew several rings of smoke in the boy's face.

He loosened the wrist restraints, ordering Dane to turn, facing the barn wall. The man placed the boy's wrists even higher so that the boy' body arched upward. His heels were off the dirt floor. With that, Dane's ass received twenty paddlings from a large Leather paddle. He cried out as the Leather paddle struck his reddened ass with increasing intensity. A Leathered fist made its entry into Dane's asshole and the boy screamed as the fist assaulted him. The fist explored every region of the boy's hole.

The Leatherman turned Dane back around and got in Dane's face.

"You piece of shit. You don't seem to understand that you are now my property, you are my slave and you will submit to my demands. I am your S&M Leatherdaddy." The man was intimidating. His frame was covered in ass-tight skins. His chest was mounded with muscle and his boots looked like they could choke the life out of a boy simply by standing on his throat. Dane realized that he must submit to the Leatherman's demands or else he would never return to his home.

"Yes, Sir, I understand, Sir. Have your way with my worthless piece of ass, Sir."

"I intend to, son," the Leatherman assured the boy, but there seemed to be a slight softness in his voice, now that Dane had acquiesced to his demands. The Leatherman continued to assault the boy's flesh.

All this time, the two boys had remained silent. The Leatherman stood in front of them, with legs firmly planted apart.

"I think you boys have done your time."

"Yes, Sir," they each replied weakly.

He released them and they fell to their knees, one licking the left boot, the other one licked the right boot.

He kicked them roughly when they had completed their task.

"You will return next weekend for a similar session, am I understood?"

"Yes, Sir. Thank you, Sir," they replied.

They beat a hasty retreat and now the boy and the Leatherman were alone in the barn.

"Just so you know, boy, they are my slaves... they have been coming here for close to three months for their Daddy's brand of punishment."

With that the Daddy unchained his boy, dragged him to a nearby bench, and roughly pushed the boy's head down between his muscular thighs. The boy massaged the man's codpiece with his tongue until he was told to pull it off with his teeth. Dane quickly fell to the task of sucking his Daddy's big, throbbing manrod. A task he really enjoyed. The boy's expensive Leathers were covered in dust and sweat, but the boy didn't care. This experience had carried him to a new plateau and the boy craved the man's attention through beatings and whippings.

He was rechained to the wall and the Leatherman worked him over for several more hours. By the end of the session, the boy's Leathers were thrown on the dirt floor. His body was covered in whip marks, spit, cigar ash and sweat.

Several days later, Dane's life was back to the way it used to be. His schedule was hectic – coursework, papers, finals, and his thesis. His whole body still ached with the S&M beatings he had received and Dane relished the feeling. But the business at hand was finishing his education..

That morning, he had an appointment at 10 o'clock with Dr. Frazier who had been forwarded a copy of the thesis draft. Frazier was the acknowledged expert on colonial through early 19th century architecture in the mid Atlantic. Word was that Dr. Frazier was a ball-breaker and many students' graduation had been delayed because of Frazier's critique. As he rushed to the office, he prayed that Frazier would like him and the draft, although his former confidence had been restored to a certain degree and he felt certain that he could bullshit with the best of them.

He knocked on the door and entered when told to do so. He lowered his eyes as he approached the formidable man.

"Sit down, son. You have written a good, solid thesis. Your study is comprehensive with the exception of the barn on my property. What do you know about it, son?"

"Not enough, Sir, but I hope that you will allow me the privilege of visiting it again this weekend."

Dr. Frazier, of course, was the Leatherman. Dane realized he must submit to the professor's demands if he was to finish his thesis. His visits continued long after the thesis was finished. The other two boys who had recently finished their degrees were there as well. It was apparent that their education was just beginning as Daddy's Leatherboys.

ABOUT THE AUTHOR

G.W. Leatherman Parks has been a Leatherman for over thirty years. He is a proud member of the Leather Archives and Museum in Chicago and writes frequently for FLAGSHIP, the newsletter of Fits Like a Glove. He has also been published in *Drummer* and *Cuir: For LeatherMen by LeatherMen*. He is a collector of vintage Leather, Leather artwork and photography.

www.ingramcontent.com/pod-product-compliance
Lightning Source LLC
Chambersburg PA
CBHW051136260626
47170CB00005B/1839